Dedication

Andrew and Trey, the loves of my life.

Justin, for reminding me that creativity is the key to life.

To Laurie, for the friendship.

Amanda, for 27 years of being the Lily to my Molly.

Momma, for giving me your strength.

Mazikeen, for reminding me that sometimes you just need to be wild.

Casper, my best friend, for calming me in the eye of a storm. I love you.

To YOU, the reader, for picking up this book and seeing life through Lily's eyes. May you find yourself in love, happy, and enjoying life the way that Lily does.

"I do not see as well without her. I do not hear as well without her. I do not feel as well without her. I would be better off without a hand or a leg than without my sister."
—Erin Morgenstern

⇒*Prologue*⇐

"Hey, sis. It's been a while, I know." I spoke while awkwardly sitting down on the blanket I'd brought along. I turned to look up at him with a smile once I was settled and he nodded, then walked away to sit on one of the benches across the cemetery. "I'm sorry. Life gets in the way sometimes, you know? There is a lot to catch up on."

I reached down to place a hand on my swollen stomach and then sighed heavily. It had been over a year since I'd visited my sister's grave and I felt, well, I felt guilty about that for some stupid reason. I knew she wouldn't care or mind at all because that's how she was.

Or I guess I should say, how she'd been when she was alive. Funny how I sometimes forgot that part when I spoke about Daisy. She'd been through so much in such a short life that I often forgot that she wasn't here anymore. I found myself looking for her around every corner still. I still felt like I needed to protect her, mostly from herself, but from a world that just didn't understand who she was or why she was two totally different people.

Daisy wasn't always Daisy. Sometimes she was Molly. Well, mostly she was Molly. Molly was who protected Daisy and kept her safe from all that she'd been through. You see, when my sister was three years old she was abducted and abused her entire formative years. She'd never had a chance at a real childhood, even after we found her.

I don't remember a lot of those first few years when she'd returned home because I was just a baby but Momma and Daddy always tell me that I loved to watch her instead of Barney on tv. They said Molly liked me a lot, even though we all knew that was a lie. She'd tried to kill me once, maybe twice but it really wasn't her fault.

"There I go, still protecting you after all this time." I spoke to her like she was here and a part of me believed she was, still watching over me and still needing me to watch over her. "Mom must have been here," I said, running a finger over the petals of a bouquet of flowers that looked fresh. "She still comes every week?"

I laughed to myself about that. Our mother, Amy, was getting up there in years now but she still faithfully visited my sister every week no matter what. I knew it had been hard on her when Daisy died. She blamed herself. She had always blamed herself for what happened to Daisy and for Molly even existing.

The years that Daisy was missing were horrible on both of my parents and I didn't even want to begin to imagine how it must have felt not knowing if your daughter was safe or even alive. Things hadn't really gotten any easier for them either after Daisy came home. Momma had a newborn baby to care for and a severely abused and traumatized child to help heal. She and Daddy had really been through it while Daisy was missing.

But after, well, after was a whole novel in and of itself. They had both fought so hard to help my sister. They'd found Dr. Morales early on and she'd been wonderful with Molly. See, it wasn't Daisy who came home, it was Molly. Dr. Morales helped us all realize that Molly was just a personality that Daisy's mind had created to protect her from the worst of the abuse that she'd suffered.

Dissociative Identity Disorder is what she'd called it. Momma called it multiple personalities and Gram, well she just said that Molly was crazy. Growing up it was hard because I never knew if I was going to get Daisy, the sweet and kind sister who loved to play dolls with me and was still so toddler like it was terrifying the older I got, or if it was going to be Molly who greeted me.

Molly was tough. She could handle anything but she also didn't handle things in the best manner. She fought. I mean physically fought. Momma was always having to go pick her up from school because she'd hit someone or pushed a kid. Molly was home more than she was in class and it aged Momma a great deal then. I know my parents did their best to be patient with her, but there was only so much patience in a person and in a family.

Teachers hated her. Kids couldn't stand her and by association me. I was ostracized for being her little sister. I'd come home crying and begging my parents to let me change my name or let me go to another school that Molly hadn't been to.

In a town as small as ours, there was no such a thing and everyone knew exactly who I was thanks to her. I'd taken my fair share of ass beatings thanks to my sister but no matter what I was there for her because she needed me. I would have done anything in the world to protect her, especially once I started to understand just a little bit about what she'd gone through.

I'll save you all the horrendous details but my sister was trafficked at a very young age and I'm sure there is still video and photos of her in some disgusting person's possession. The monsters who did that to her have paid their price and both are dead now. I hope they are somewhere feeling twice the pain and horror that she felt as a small child. They stole her innocence, her childhood and her soul. Unfortunately for Daisy, she would continue to fight the demons that had become the norm for her. She spent her life trapped inside a prison that those monsters created for her and she wasn't able to break free.

Once I hit my teens I knew that something was terribly wrong with her but she refused to get help. She wouldn't even speak to our parents. I think a little part of her blamed momma for letting her get taken. Not that Momma could have stopped it or even done anything differently. It wasn't something she did or didn't do. It just happened and Daisy was gone in the blink of an eye.

Of course, Momma blamed herself. And Daddy, well, I think he blamed her too. The way he looked at her sometimes, it filled me with pure terror. I could see his mind flashing back to that awful day when she'd told him that Daisy was gone. How he didn't hate her was unfathomable to me but he'd stayed through it all. That kind of thing can rip a marriage and a family apart but Daddy put aside any blame or thought of blame and stayed by momma's side through the end.

She always believed that Daisy would come home. She never wavered in her belief that someday her little girl would return and they'd be a family again. She'd been right of course but it wasn't Daisy who came home. It was Molly and Molly wasn't the same sweet little girl that had been abducted.

But I'm getting ahead of myself here. I guess I should have started with "Hi, I'm Lily and my sister killed herself after a horrible battle with DID and depression."

That about sums it up, I guess.

I was sixteen when she died. Sixteen and the only one she confided in. I did my best to help her, even down to betraying her and telling our parents what was going on so she could get the help she so badly needed.

I'm pretty sure she hated me for that but I didn't care at the time. My sister was in trouble and I didn't want to lose her. In the end, we all lost her. Molly did her best to protect Daisy. She did everything she could but once the two were integrated, it became too much. Daisy had never dealt with the abuse because Daisy hadn't lived through it. That was Molly. And Molly, well, Molly just held on. It was all she could do.

I turned my attention back to the headstone that read "Daisy Renee Anders. She was loved by us."

And just below that it read "Molly Renee Anders. She gave her all to protect Daisy".

I often wondered how many people read that and thought that there were two people beneath their feet. I guess in some way there was. They were two very different people for sure.

"I guess you're wondering what kept me away, huh?" Speaking to her seemed as natural as breathing. "Well I've been a little busy. Jason and I got married but you knew that. What you don't know is that he got a new job and we moved. We're closer to Mom and Dad now but I guess that is a good thing with the twins coming next month. Oh yeah, we are expecting twins. Found out yesterday that we're having two little girls. I wanted you to know because we've decided to name them Daisy and Molly in honor of their auntie. I hope you'll be okay with that. I know that neither of those names ever really felt right to you but I wanted a small part of you still here, Daisy. I miss you so much. No matter how much time passes it's never enough to take away that empty feeling of you not being here."

I glanced back over at Jason, who was looking anywhere but at me. Bless this man that had come into my life. His childhood was almost as fucked up as mine and we spent many nights trying to outdo one another with tales of how bad our lives growing up had been. Some nights he won, others I did. It all depended on which stories we told. When I really wanted to win I told the story of how my dearly departed sister tried to murder me.

Not that she really wanted to succeed. Or at least I don't think that she did. She was young and I was just a little kid and momma swore it was an accident. But I'd spent the night in the hospital and so had Molly. It was definitely Molly who stayed in that hospital. I heard her screaming at the nurses all night long once she woke up. Molly was mad at everyone and everything and it worried me even then.

I guess none of this makes sense right now to anyone but me so I should probably stop talking and start back at the beginning.

Chapter One

My name is Lily Anders and my sister was abducted at the age of three years old. I was born the very night they found her nine years later. Talk about a weight to carry. Growing up as the sister of the kidnapped girl wasn't easy but clearly I survived. It wasn't like I had a choice in the matter because someone had to protect her.

That's exactly what I did my entire life. I protected Daisy, aka Molly. Sometimes I think it's why I was born on that exact day. It was as if the Universe knew that she'd need me from the very moment she was saved.

I had a pretty normal childhood except for the whole abused and trafficked sister part. My parents loved me and took good care of me. They were a little overprotective but I couldn't blame them for that given what had happened to our family. I don't even know how to explain it.

Except that it happened. I've heard the story so many times and it's why Momma never let me out of her sight anywhere. She'd put Daisy down to look at the fish in Walmart. She turned her back for one second to grab cat food and when she looked back, Daisy was gone.

It wasn't something anyone expected in our tiny little Upstate New York town. We lived in the valley at the foot of a mountain and we had one traffic light. The only thing to do on a Friday night was go out to eat for either an expensive steak on Main Street or to the diner down the street. No one ever even dreamed that someone would come into our WalMart and steal a child.

The police sure didn't know how to help my momma. They bumbled things from the beginning if you asked me. The only one with any sense at all was Detective Witte and she was about as bright as a 40 watt light bulb. I mean, she helped my parents out a lot, especially my mother. Detective Witte was the one who sat with her those first few nights, when she didn't sleep and cried the entire night. Momma used to talk about how she felt so helpless those first few days.

"I just wanted her to come home," she told me every time she told the story.

That's just what it was to me when I was little. A story. I didn't really understand that my sister was the kid and my momma was the lady who cried until I was about seven. That's when the lightbulb went off in my brain and made me realize that Molly was the Molly who lived in my house.

I used to hear her crying some nights and I never understood why until then. It would be many more years before I even knew the full story of all that had happened to her. I admired her strength and her ability to survive. Molly could do anything. She could be anything. She was tough and smart.

Daisy, on the other hand, was quiet and shy where Molly was loud and in your face. Daisy stayed to herself. She didn't have any friends. Molly was the life of the party.

It was hard at first to understand why my sister was two different people. I still don't fully understand how it all worked but Momma and Daddy said that no matter who she was, she was their daughter and my sister and we loved her.

I did love her. I loved Molly and Daisy. They were both my sister and I didn't want anything or anyone to ever hurt her again.

One thing that I will never forget is the first time I can remember Molly cutting herself. I didn't know what was happening but Momma was screaming and there was blood everywhere. Momma kept asking her why over and over. Molly just quietly spoke, barely above a whisper.

"I just want the outside to match the inside" she said as if it was the most logical thing in the world.

That stuck with me my whole life. Can you even imagine how she must have felt on the inside to think that the only way the outside could match was to take a knife to your flesh and cut as deep as you can?

I remember the first time I told my therapist this story and she told me that sometimes people get so hurt or traumatized that only more pain can make them feel better. She said that for them, the pain makes them feel like they are alive.

The things that Molly endured were so horrific that I didn't even know most of them until after she took her own life. I was only seventeen then but I'd been taking care of her for years. So much so that I visited every week at the very least so I could make sure she had groceries in her apartment and she'd paid her rent and light bill.

She forgot those things so easily. Her mind was so twisted up with all the memories that haunted her from those years she was missing. I honestly don't know if I would have survived had it been me that was taken and not her.

My therapist said that Molly had lived through a war and she was forever scarred mentally and physically by it. I started to look at her differently after that. I no longer saw the sister who couldn't handle her own life. In her place I saw a young woman who had been sexually and physically abused from the age of three until nine. I saw a woman who had survived the worst things a child could be subjected to and she was alive and she was living her life. That was so powerful to me. She was powerful.

I only wish she'd felt even a little bit of the pride I felt knowing that she'd survived all of that. I don't think that she believed she was worthy of love or of being alive. Whatever that horrible man and woman had done to her had fucked her up beyond repair.

They say that abuse victims often believe that they don't deserve better because their abuser has convinced them of it. The psychological impact of abuse is astounding to me. How did she survive? I mean, I know that her mind created a whole other identity. I fully understand that part. What I don't understand is how her brain even knew how to do that. How did Daisy just get pushed to the back and Molly become the one in charge?

I learned early on that Molly existed to protect Daisy no matter the cost. In the end, it cost her everything. But when we were younger, Molly was the most fun. She was willing to do anything and she took me along with her on those adventures. Molly never let me get hurt or lost. She watched me like a hawk and if she even thought someone was looking at me wrong, she was there, ready to fight.

When the kids at school picked on me or made fun of me, Molly was there. When I got my heart broken for the first time, Molly was there. She held me and let me cry then she dried my tears and told me to toughen up. She didn't say it to be mean. She was trying to teach me to be strong and I appreciate that now more than ever.

Molly never let me down.

Daisy was….different. She was shy and quiet. She never really looked anyone in the eye and all she ever wanted to do was stay home and read. Not that there was anything wrong with wanting to read but she never wanted to leave the house period.

The doctors all told us that Daisy didn't have a clue about what had happened to her but I didn't really buy that. There was a reason she never wanted to leave home. I think she knew but she chose to pack it away deep inside her mind, in the places that only Molly lived. That was how she coped and it wasn't the best coping mechanism at all.

In spite of all of that, Daisy was kind and generous. She always helped Momma with the dishes or with cooking dinner. She never complained, not even when she had the flu. She just got up and continued on with her daily life. We didn't even know she was sick until the teacher called to say that Daisy had had a rough few days and wanted to know if anything was going on at home.

It wasn't but how did my parents explain to a teacher that Daisy was kind and quiet because she'd been abused? Of course we all understood that everyone in town knew what had happened to Daisy all those years she was gone. We also understood that people didn't say anything because they felt bad for our family.

Sometimes I wondered why those same people always stared at Molly when we were out. They treated her like she was some kind of monster that they just wanted to see up close and personal. Momma was always kind to people but Daddy often forgot and lost his temper with them.

He hated how people treated Molly. She wasn't a freak. She was just a little girl who had been through so much and he wanted her to have a normal childhood now that she was home.

Normal wasn't really something any of us really understood. We weren't a normal family by any means. Momma and Daddy basically had to keep the house locked down at all times to avoid the press that camped outside of our house anytime someone on some true crime podcast mentioned our family. Momma listened to them all relentlessly so she could try to get them to stop talking about Molly. She hadn't had much luck.

One of those podcasts called and wanted them to do a segment and just out of the blue Momma decided to do it. The ladies from "People Are the Worst" showed up on a Friday evening and stayed until the following week.

Rachel and Rebecca were different from every other media person that had reached out to them. They were respectful and kind, spending a lot of time talking to Molly and myself. They asked a few questions but mostly they just listened when Momma or Daddy talked about what it had been like when Molly was missing.

They didn't pry or even want the salacious details of what happened to Molly. They just wanted to know her story and tell it in a respectful way. Daddy had been furious with Momma when she'd told him that she'd agreed but by the end of their visit, he knew that they'd help others.

And that is what it was all about for our parents. They never wanted another family to go through what we'd gone through. Momma lobbied to get stricter laws passed and pressed for harsher sentences for crimes against children. Daddy volunteered any time there was a missing person case in our area and sometimes even out of state. They worked tirelessly to change the world so that it would be safe for the Molly's of the world.

All while Molly was slowly losing her way. It didn't happen overnight. She slowly started to change. She'd always been a little hard around the edges but it was around the time that she entered high school that she really wilded out. She started hanging out with the druggies and the losers. She wore all black and rarely spoke to any of us. I was still a little kid then but I knew that something was wrong with her.

Back then, she hated me. She hated that I had the childhood she was robbed of and honestly, I probably would have hated me too. It obviously wasn't my fault, or hers.

I know what you're thinking. You're thinking that I make a lot of excuses for my sister. You're right. I do. Wouldn't you? Think about it. Think about all that she lived through and how you'd react to that. It wasn't easy for any of us but it was the hardest on Molly.

Truly, I am in awe of how she survived it at all and how she managed to be as well adjusted as she was. Even with everything that had happened in her short life, she still loved openly and gave willingly. That speaks more about my sister than anything else I could say.

At the end of the day, she was a human being who had been through hell and survived to tell the tale. I'm not so sure I'd have been able to make it as long as she did. Not after what that monster did to her. I've never spoken his name and I never will. When he died I begged Momma to take me to his grave. She refused but when I was fifteen, Molly and I went. She wanted to see for herself that he was gone and would never hurt her or anyone else again. I had other reasons for going.

As we stood there, I spit on his grave. I asked God to let him spend an eternity feeling everything my sister felt. I wanted him to feel everything he'd ever done to her and the others.

Yes, there were others. Molly found them years after she'd come home and she called them her family. Our family accepted each and every one of them because they were all Molly to us. Each one had their own horror story to tell about what he'd done to them and together they found a way to heal some of the pain. The wounds would always be there but the pain could lessen and it was good for them.

Sadly, Molly wasn't the only one of them who had taken their own lives. We attended many of their funerals over the years and Momma cried for everyone of them. She hugged their mothers, held their hands, and listened to countless stories of their lives. She supported and loved each and every parent that had lost a child.

She'd come home late in the evening and just hug Molly and I. She constantly reminded Molly of how much we loved her and how strongly we fought for her. It annoyed Molly but I saw that small look of hope in her eyes that what our mother told her was true.

My sister didn't believe she was worthy of being loved. Maybe that was the saddest part of her entire story. She believed what that monster did to her made her undeserving of the basic human desire to be loved by her family.

I loved my sister. I loved her in spite of what had been done to her. I loved her for the kindness I knew she had and the fear that kept her awake at night. I loved her for her tough exterior and the tears she shed when she thought no one was looking. She was my big sister. She was who I looked to when I needed a friend. She was Molly and Daisy and I loved her in any form she took.

Chapter Two

When Molly moved out, our world changed. No longer was I "Molly's little sister". I became Lily Anders, person. My parents expected more out of me because I hadn't been abducted as a child. I didn't get away with things that Molly or Daisy did. She got a free pass a lot of the time and it really made me angry some days. Those were the days I went to see her. Those visits always put things into perspective for me.
My life was easy compared to my sister's. I had friends I could count on, parents who loved me, and I didn't have this mental illness that made me struggle every day. Of course I had my sad days but they didn't even compare to Molly's sad days.

On my sad days I stayed home and read or called a friend and vented. On her sad days she self-destructed. The world stopped spinning in her universe on those days. It was terrifying to watch her then. Unlike everyone else who is having a bad day and stays in bed, Molly partied. Molly slept around. Molly did drugs to forget. Molly lost track of time and herself.

Those days were spent picking her up off the floor. Most days she'd wake up not knowing where she was or what she'd done. She spiraled on those days and I was the only one she trusted back then. Those were the years that she didn't speak to our parents. She'd started to believe the bullshit that that asshole who took her had fed her all those years she was missing.

She believed that my parents had given her to him, that they'd approved of what he'd done to her all those years. It made no sense at all to any of us but we didn't live with the trauma and the triggers that Molly did. My parents hated that Molly felt that way but they didn't push as hard as they could have. They'd both spent so many years in therapy and in group therapy that they understood that traumatic events really messed up your mind especially when they happened in your formative years.

I remember Momma used to tell Molly that she should forgive him and herself because it would free her from the mental jail that she lived in. Molly wasn't ready to forgive. I didn't blame her one little bit. Forgiveness is really hard to do when you've been hurt so badly that you're scarred for life.

I hated him almost as much as Molly. He'd stolen my big sister from me. Even though I didn't know her prior to the abduction I do know that had it not happened our relationship would have been a lot different. Maybe instead of me protecting Molly, she could have protected me.

It would have been nice to be the little sister and have a big sister who wasn't so fucked up that she was barely surviving. It would have been a hell of a lot easier to not have to deal with any of this.

Sometimes, when I was all alone I thought about how things would have been without her ever coming home. What if I'd never known her? Would my life be easier? Would my parents be happier? What if Molly had never been found?

Chapter Three

I hated to admit that I thought of that often. What if Molly hadn't been found? What if she had died or they just never found her?

What if, on the day that I was born, my parents gave up trying to find her?
Did that make me a horrible person? Should I be ashamed of thinking things like that? I would never tell my parents or my sister that I thought about it like that. Usually it only happened after Molly spiraled out of control. Those were tough times and honestly, at sixteen years old, I should never have been expected to pick her up off the floor she would eventually wind up on.

I should have been dating, going to football games, and having fun with my friends. Instead, I was babysitting my mentally unstable and traumatized sister. That just seemed to be my lot in life.

My parents expected me to help Molly when she needed help. I didn't really get much choice in it since I was the only family member that Molly still spoke to. That's how I wound up spending my weekends sleeping on my sister's couch instead of being passed out drunk in a field with my friends. It was hard to be passed out in a field when your sister was the one passed out, usually in a field, and usually underneath some guy.

Molly was a whore. Even she said it. Daisy was shy and quiet. I wondered if Daisy even knew how many men had used her body. I doubted it because Daisy wasn't out all that often. She seemed to not mind that Molly was in charge of her life. I think she actually preferred it that way.

Molly spent so much of her time stoned out of her mind that she really didn't deal with anything that was happening to her. When she was sober, she was sad. When she was sad, she wanted to die. It was a vicious cycle that we all wished we could get out of but until Molly admitted she needed help from someone other than me, we were stuck right here.

Dr. Morales did her best to help but she could only do so much when Molly missed more sessions than she attended. Justin and the others from her group that had been abused by the same man tried their best to get through to Molly. When Daisy was in charge, she agreed to therapy and to being committed until they could integrate her and Molly but Molly never let that happen.

Each and every time she pushed through and took over. Momma and Daddy tried to 5150 her but the judge refused to sign it because he felt sorry for Molly. He did her more harm than good with that sympathy. She'd have been much better off spending some time in an institution than where she was.

There were more than a few nights that she slept on the street because she couldn't find her way home. She even spent a few nights in a jail cell after being picked up for soliciting an undercover cop. This was the life my sister led.

I couldn't place too much blame on her with all that she'd been through as a child but at the same time I wanted her to see that she was self-destructing. She needed more help than I could give her. I was just a teenager after all.

She just couldn't see it though. I don't know if she didn't want to or if she was just oblivious to the fact that she was the adult and I was the child. It was like living with a neglectful parent some days.

Momma and Daddy tried their best to get me to let her make her mistakes and pay the consequences but I couldn't turn my back on her. Everyone in her life had done that. She'd been hurt by every single person except for me.

I fought alone to keep her safe. I wanted her to know that one person in the world loved her for who she was, no matter who she was. My friends never understood how I could keep choosing to subject myself to Molly. They all begged me to forget about her and hang out all the time. I couldn't. I couldn't abandon her. She was my sister after all.

That may not have meant anything to her or anyone else but it meant everything to me. I loved her. It was second nature to me to be there for Molly. Most days I felt that I was born to do just that because out of everyone in the world, Molly needed me.

Don't get me wrong, I knew that my parents loved me and that they'd wanted to have me. I understood that I wasn't a replacement for Daisy. My grandparents had no idea that I'd overheard them saying that to my mom and dad. To my parents' credit, they shut that down immediately. Daddy was beyond pissed off when they said that. He screamed at Gran, telling her that they'd never thought of trying to replace their daughter with another child. He brought up the fact that prior to Daisy being taken they'd often talked about having another baby and so when Momma found herself pregnant they'd been overjoyed.

Of course they had missed Daisy. She was their daughter, their firstborn child and they would never have stopped looking for her.

After they'd left, Daddy told Momma that they weren't welcome in his house again. He then stormed off to check on Daisy/Molly. I heard Momma crying in her room later and I snuck in to hug her.

It was the very first thing I remembered about my grandparents. I only ever saw them again at their house and Daddy never went along. He refused to even go to Grampa's funeral a few years later.

I can't remember another time that my father was ever that mad at anyone. He was a great dad and always made a point of giving me extra hugs and took time to spend one on one time with me.

When I was seven, I begged and begged my momma for a cat but she had said no multiple times. One night, Daddy came home with a tiny little orange kitten and handed her straight to me. I squealed with happiness and named her immediately. I named her James and Molly told me that was the dumbest name in the entire world.

I burst out crying and Daddy sent her to her room without dessert for the night. Daddy always had my back but Molly was so mad that she destroyed her room that evening. Of course after that, Momma had to hug her and help her calm down. It didn't matter that she'd been mean to me or that she'd made me cry. Momma always took Molly's side, no matter what.

I learned in therapy years later that she was trying to make up for all the time she'd lost with her. Momma always went out of her way to make Molly feel accepted and loved. She rarely raised her voice or punished Molly.

I should be angry with her, especially now, but I wasn't. A part of me understood why she did it. Now that I was about to have children, I understood it. I would do anything to make sure my children were happy. I couldn't blame my mother for what she'd done to help Molly readjust to life inside a normal family and a normal life.

It took a lot of my mother's strength to take care of a child who had been abused the way my sister had been. I don't think anyone understood what my mother had to endure when Molly came home.

I know she wasn't prepared for it. She'd just had a baby. She'd just had me. She had so many hormones and emotions rushing through her and then she had to deal with a nine year old, heavily traumatized nine year old child. She had no idea the kind of life Molly had had to deal with back then. She was simply happy that her daughter would be coming home.

She knew so little then and she had a brand new baby who was going to take a lot of her energy and time. No one could have prepared her for how much time and attention Molly would require too.

She used to talk about how tired she'd been back then like it was a medal of honor. She was cautious to mention how much Daddy had helped her then. She appreciated him and all he did for his family.

They had a marriage that was filled with love and respect. Of course they had their fights and problems. All marriages did or so they often reminded me. When Jason and I first started to get serious, they sat us down and told us all about how relationships and marriages were not meant to be perfect but they were meant to be cherished and worked at.

I think that they knew then that Jason and I would marry. We didn't but it had worked out the way it was meant to in the end.

I met Jason towards the end of Molly's life. Things were bad and I was struggling to help her and I was distracted most of the time. It was then that I literally bumped into him. Of course I didn't know at that moment how much he'd come to mean to me or how he'd save me after my sister died.

What I did know then was that he was the most beautiful man I'd ever seen in my entire life. He grabbed my arm and stopped me from falling and I fell in love at that moment. He asked me out that day and I said yes because why wouldn't I?

Funny how one moment in time can change your whole life. We were inseparable after that. I spent every second I could with him. He was graduating that year and had already been accepted to Fordham University which meant he would be leaving after the summer was over. That feeling of not being able to see him everyday was nearly enough to break my heart. He kissed me and held me that night and reminded me that he loved me. He insisted that nothing would change between us but I was a realist and I knew that it would. I could only hope that he wouldn't find someone else at college.

I'm sure you've figured out that he didn't but it wasn't always easy. Molly drove him crazy. He wasn't her biggest fan and I couldn't blame him. He hadn't been there when she came home. He didn't know everything. I didn't want to tell him. I didn't want him to look at me differently. I wanted him to love me. I didn't want him knowing how she needed me.

I didn't want him to know her. I didn't want him to see her when she spiraled out of control. I didn't want him to judge her because he would be right and I'd have to defend her when I didn't believe that she had the right to behave the way she did. Maybe that made me a bad sister or a bad person but I didn't care. She'd had too many years to work through her trauma and deal with her past and she hadn't done it.

I sounded bitter even to myself but that's how I felt and what I thought and I couldn't change it. I wanted my sister to be better. I wanted her to be happy and find someone to love and have a family. And I wanted her to never be abducted or abused or anything else horrible that has ever happened to her.

I also wanted her to not sleep around or do drugs. I wanted her to eat every day and sleep in her own bed every night. I wanted so much more for her but I didn't know how to help her get all of those things.

At some point she would have to help herself. I had serious doubts that she could but if it ever happened I'd be right there to hug her and tell her how proud I was of her.

But Jason, he didn't need to be part of this madness that came with Molly. She could destroy him with her life easily and I'd be damned if I'd let her world mix with his.

Jason was the best man and he treated me like I deserved being loved. Of course, I had already filled him in on my sister and everything our family had been through. I just hadn't told him about how much she was still causing us all issues. He would have demanded that I immediately tell my parents how bad things were and I'd promised Molly that I wouldn't get them involved unless I felt her life was in danger.

That day was fast approaching I feared but until then I would honor my promise to her.

I leaned in to run my hand over the smooth marble of my sister's headstone. I traced her name over and over for a few minutes, tears welling up in my eyes. For a few brief moments I couldn't breathe. Every time I came here it all hit me like it had the day Momma had called me to tell me she was gone. The pain was harsh.

It felt like someone had reached right into my chest, pulled my heart out and left a gaping hole. I could still feel it beating, echoing throughout my entire soul and yet it had stopped the day she died.

I wanted her back. I needed her back. The good. The bad. The worse. I needed Molly back so that the world made sense again.

"Damn it Molly, I want to hate you for dying. I want to hate you for destroying me by dying. It wasn't supposed to be this way. None of this is right in any way at all. You should be here to help me with the girls, to sit with me and hold my hand. You've missed so much. You weren't there for my wedding. I didn't even have a maid of honor because it was meant for you. I had no one stand there with me, just emptiness, like my life since you've been gone. Why? Why did you do it, Molly?"

I sat there, my hand resting on her name, trying to catch my breath as the pain hit me once more. I knew why she'd done it. I knew full well the Hell she'd lived through and suffered through. I knew how fucked up she was and how hard she tried to hide it. She didn't have much luck with the hiding it part but she tried her best.

I wish I had been there for her in those last moments. I would have told her how much I loved her and needed her. I would have held her and comforted her in those last moments of her life. I hated that she was alone and didn't know that she had so much to live for. No matter how much she apologized to me in her note, I'd never forgive her for leaving me here.

Maybe I was insane to sit here, seven months pregnant, talking to my dead sister. To Jason's credit he didn't question me at all. Perhaps he was sitting there wondering when his wife had lost her mind. Or maybe he was wondering if he could take the babies after they were born and leave me to save them from the insanity that would be life with me for a mother.

I glanced over at him and smiled at how at peace he looked sitting there. Our lives were going to change drastically in a few short weeks but he loved me and I loved him. Maybe it was better that Molly was gone. Would we have been able to trust leaving her alone with the girls even for a few minutes?

I held onto that thought and hated myself for thinking it while I was sitting here talking to her grave. She wasn't here to defend herself and I was making her out to be a horrible human being. I guess she wasn't all that great when she was alive.

But it wasn't her fault. Nothing that had happened to her was her fault. I'd told myself that for years but in reality it wasn't all true. Yes, what had happened to her as a child wasn't her fault. What she'd done as an adult had been Molly's choice and she made bad choices. There were times she tried her best to be better. She went to therapy. She went to group. She talked to Momma and Daddy. She showed up for family dinners and family events. She came to Christmas dinner and made an effort to be a normal human. It never lasted long.

I hated that I judged her so much. She didn't need judgment. She needed understanding and here I was sitting at her grave judging her.

Momma would tell me that I had every right to judge her since I knew her the best and I'd been the one to take care of her when she was at her worst. Daddy would tell me to stop dwelling on the past and let Molly stay dead.

Maybe he was right? Maybe I should let her stay dead. Could I actually do that? Would I do that? Would Molly really stay dead?

I didn't have the answers to any of that and I didn't think I'd find them any time soon. Jason would tell me to follow my heart but how could I do that when I had no idea what my heart wanted? Most days it wanted to not feel like it was being ripped out of my chest. That's exactly why I stayed away from the graveyard.

The babies didn't need the stress. Twins were already hard enough without having to be stressed all the time. I wasn't really sure how I would have been able to take care of my sister and the babies. There was no way I would have been able to handle it all and not lose my mind.

Maybe she knew what she was doing. Had she thought about the rest of us before she did it? Was it intentional or a mistake? Did she mean to do it? Why? Why then? What had happened then that drove her to this?

She'd met London and fallen in love. They were so good together. He loved her. He loved her for all of her misadventures and all of her craziness. He wanted nothing more than to love her for the rest of his life and the next. She was his soulmate he'd once told me. He learned how to handle her bouts of depression and when Daisy was out, he learned how to be her friend and not let her know what Molly had done. Molly had begged him to never tell Daisy what had happened to them.

Molly had told him everything. She'd filled him in on things she told no one. Molly trusted London more than she trusted me. At first that hurt but then I figured it out. There were things she felt that she couldn't tell me. She was protecting me in her own way. I should have been angry with her but for once she put me before herself.

For once, Molly was my big sister. Was that what she was being when he took her own life? Was she protecting me or herself? Did it really matter anymore?

The answer to that was a resounding yes.

Chapter Four

"I don't know if I should hate you or be grateful," I said to her tombstone. "Hating you would be so easy. Loving you was so damn hard. What would it be like now if you were still here? Would you and London be married? Would you have pushed him away like you did everyone else?

He's married now, you know? They have a daughter. He named her Molly. I don't know that his wife really liked it but how could she say no to him given the circumstances? He still loves you. She knows that she was his second choice and had you still been alive, she would never have had a chance with him. We get together every year on your birthday and the day you died. He still talks about you like you're going to walk through the door any minute. I worry about him. He never got over you being gone."

London had been so good for her. He'd brought her out of the darkness and shined a light on her. She lived with him. Not in the same house type of living. I mean, she was alive with him. He made her feel safe and she needed that more than anything else in her life. He was there for the good times and the bad. He held her hand and challenged her. He breathed life into her. He gave her unconditional love and made her feel worthy of it. They were good together and in her own way, Molly loved him. She smiled every time she mentioned his name. She introduced him to our mother. She was in love with him.

They'd met in some weird way that she did her best to tell me all about but I wasn't sure that I understood anything she said to me. To this day I still don't really know how they met. Both of them told me a different story each time I saw them together. It was a game to them and they found it quite funny. I did not.

London loved my sister and had become a very good friend to me as well. We made a point of having lunch a few times a year since Molly's death. He'd even invited me to his wedding when he got married a few years ago. Jason and I went but it didn't seem right to me that I was there. He should have married my sister. They should be the one with the child and living happily ever after.

"I can't believe he actually married someone other than you. She's really nice though. Pretty in a plain girl kind of way. She's smart and quiet and she has her life all figured out. I can't help but to wonder if you and London would have been married by now. Would you have babies? Would you have been a good mother?"

My mind wandered and I grimaced when the babies moved and flipped. They were running out of room in there and I was beyond ready for this all to be over.

We met up with my parents later that evening at the diner. We hadn't been to visit in a few months and my mother fawned all over me making a huge fuss over how big I was now. I hated that she pointed it out but I understood how excited she was to be a grandmother. She was born to take care of little babies. I knew that she never forgave herself for what happened to Molly. She blamed herself and nothing anyone of us said helped her move past that.

She had been the one to find Molly after. It had been even harder on her than Molly getting abducted. She blamed herself for that too. Daddy had come to her immediately when she called to tell him that Molly was being taken to the hospital. Neither of them left the hospital that night even after the doctor told them she was gone. My mother went straight to the chapel and prayed the entire night. Daddy sat just outside the door and waited for her.

He never stepped foot in the chapel but he made sure that she had all the time she needed to mourn and pray. He sat with his head in his hands and cried silently. His heart was broken. In fact it was shattered.

Now that I sat across from him at the dinner table, I saw that same sadness in his eyes. It had been so many years since that night and yet, it hung on his face like an antique mirror on a wall. For the first time I noticed the lines that crossed his face. They were deep and each one of them defined a moment his heart was broken by Molly.

I reached across the table and put my hand on his just because I could. At the touch he looked up and smiled at me. Daddy had always taken care of me when my heart was broken and now it was my turn to take care of him. I couldn't do it when Molly died because I was lost in my own grief but now I could be there for him and I would.

Dinner was filled with laughter and talk about the babies. Momma and Daddy planned to visit the moment they made their arrival. Jason promised he'd call them the moment we were on the way to the hospital. I sat back and just listened. This was my family, my tribe.

Everyone at this table loved me and these little girls. They all loved that I honored my sister with their names and they all supported me in everything I ever had wanted to do in my life. They cheered me on when I won and cried with me when I lost. I loved them all so very much.

So why did I feel so sad?

Because my sister wasn't here. She wasn't here for the important events in my life. I hated that she wasn't here. Losing her had been hard on all of us. Except Jason. He never knew her the way we did. He only heard the stories of her life that we'd shared with him.

He knew that she'd been the one person in the world that could destroy me with one word but would pick me up off the floor when my world fell apart. Now that was his job and he wasn't nearly as competent as she was.

I know I've talked a lot about Molly but so much of my life had revolved around hers. She was the sun and I was the planets that orbited around her.

I'd spent so much of my life in her shadow that I still felt like I lived there. Except she was gone and I was here so there was no shadow anymore for me to hide in. I had to live life on my own two feet and on my own terms.

I'd married Jason and was having babies very soon. I wasn't a child anymore. I wasn't Molly's sister anymore.

I was Lily.

And I was alive.

Chapter Five

The babies made their debut three weeks later. They came into the world screaming and within mere minutes of one another. Molly screamed as if her world had imploded around her while Daisy yawned and stretched. They'd been named perfectly.

Molly was slightly bigger at 5 pounds 2 ounces and 17 inches long. Daisy weighed in at 4 pounds 8 ounces and 15 inches. Both had blue eyes and blonde hair. They got that from my mother, the blonde hair and blue eyes.

I had my father's strawberry blonde hair and green eyes. Molly had looked just like our mother, both beautiful and tall. I felt like I faded into the darkness around them both.

Jason made me feel seen and loved. He told me all the time how beautiful I was and how much he desired me. He took care of me and made sure I ate more than once a day. He limited my coffee intake and forced me to eat veggies every single day. He was a great man and I was lucky to have married such a man.

He stood holding our daughters, smiling proudly as he sang quietly to them. He refused to put them down and had one in each arm. I laid back and closed my eyes for a few moments while I had the chance.

I woke up a few hours later and instantly sat up, looking for my babies. Jason laughed out loud at me and handed me Daisy. I held her close and inhaled her scent. She smelled of innocence, powder, and Jason.

'You've been holding them all day haven't you?" I glared at him in pretend anger and we both burst out laughing.

"I'm allowed to, Lily. I'm there dad."

"You'll spoil them."

"I don't care. They deserve to be spoiled, Lil. Look at them."

"Jason, I don't care if you spoil them. Hell I plan to do exactly that myself. Now, give me Molly."

He handed me our other daughter and I pressed a kiss to the top of her head. She smelled just like her sister and I smiled at them both.

"I swear that I'll always protect you and I'll never let the world destroy you. I'll tell you all about your namesakes when you're old enough and I'll help you understand why she isn't here to help you when you need someone like her. I will love you so fiercely that you'll never spend a single moment wondering if you were wanted."

I whispered to them, cautiously glancing over at Jason, who appeared to be involved in his phone. When I finished speaking, I sat quietly looking at them with love and awe. I didn't even notice Jason had moved until he pressed the kiss to my forehead.

"Our girls are so lucky to have you," he whispered. "I love you, Lily."

"I love you too," I said behind tears. This was our family. It was the family I had always dreamed of and I prayed that nothing would ever destroy it.

Chapter Six

Time seemed to move at lightning speed after the birth and before we knew it the girls were three months old. Jason was going back to work soon and I'd be home alone with them for the first time ever.

And I was scared out of my mind that I'd break one or both of them. It sounded silly even to me but there were two of them and they could easily gang up on me. I was outnumbered.

So when my mother called and asked about coming to stay, I jumped at the chance to have her there with me. Jason and I had talked about her staying but we'd wanted time to bond with them on our own so she'd only come for a few days right after they were born.

I knew she wanted to know them and I wanted her to be there and be present in their lives. Inviting her to stay was the right thing to do at the time. I had no idea it would end so badly.

The first week was great. Momma was a big help around the house and with the girls. She obviously loved them very much and I was thankful for her help. By the second week it felt like my mother had taken over and I was no longer the mom of my own twins. She could be bossy and I knew I needed to speak up and let her know how I wanted things done but she was my mother and a part of me was too scared to do that.

I told Jason late one night that I wanted her to go home. He looked at me like I'd lost my damn mind.

"I don't need her here, Jason."

"Lily, think about what you're saying. If she leaves, you'll be all alone with the babies. Are you sure you're ready for that?"

"Yes, I am ready. They're my babies, Jason. Not hers. She's taken over everything. I can't even feed my own children, Jason. I am their mother, not her."

"Lily," he spoke quietly. "Lower your voice. Your mother will hear you."

"I don't care." I said it so matter of factly that he stared at me in disbelief.

"Okay, what's really going on? You've said my name multiple times in one sentence so don't even try to tell me that you're fine."

"I'm not fine. Not even in the slightest. I just want to be able to care for our daughters and move past this feeling I'm feeling."

"Talk to me, baby." He pleaded, his voice breaking with worry.

"I am talking to you, Jason. I don't know what you want me to say. I want to be their mother. I want her to go home. I want my house back. I want our family to be just us right now."

"You're going to hurt her so badly if you tell her that. She loves the girls and it's possible she needs to be here right now."

I sighed heavily and frowned. "I know. That's what worries me the most. She's replacing Molly with the girls and she can't do that. She can't do it over. They aren't her babies. They're mine."

"Baby, I know this. You know this. She knows this. She just wants to help you with the girls."

"Stop trying to stop me from wanting to be alone with my husband and my babies."

I threw the pillow at him and shot him a pissed off look. I was angry and I wanted to stay angry. It was my right and I intended to take full advantage of it. He laughed and shook his head.

"We will pick up this discussion in the morning. It's time for bed. The girls will be up in a few short hours and I have an early meeting in the morning."

"Ugh! I hate when you have early meetings."

He leaned over and kissed me gently, "I know, baby. Good night. I love you."

"I love you too," I said to his already snoring back. That man could fall asleep faster than anyone I'd ever known.

I slid closer to him and closed my eyes, drifting off to sleep almost as quickly as he did. Two hours later I was wide awake as soon as the girls started crying for their midnight feedings.

I padded to the nursery and picked up Molly then Daisy holding both close to me and breathing in their scent. This was my happy place and I held them tightly to me.

I laid Molly down and changed Daisy's diaper then switched and changed Molly. By then the bottles were warm so I put them both down into their bouncy seats, taking a seat on the carpeted floor between them to hold their bottles.

I sang softly to them as they ate and watched their beautiful little features as they ate. Once they drained their bottles, Daisy yawned and closed her eyes while Molly reached out and grabbed my finger.

These were my girls. Jason and I had created them from our love for one another. They were a mixture of us both and my heart swelled with love for my husband and our girls.

This was the family that I'd longed for and yet there was a piece missing. I hated that even in the serene and happy moments my thoughts turned to her. She had ruled my life for so many years when she was alive and now, even in death, she had a stranglehold on everything I held dear.

I tried to stop the thoughts from ruining my mood and watched as my baby girls settled back in to sleep. They were perfect and nothing could spoil that.

I was still standing beside their crib watching them sleep when Momma came in. She put a hand on my shoulder and smiled at me.

"You did good, Lily. I"m so proud of you."

"Thanks, Momma." I said but didn't really feel grateful that night.

"I know it's hard for you. I know that things have never been easy and you've had so much put on your small shoulders at such a young age but you have to know how important you were and are. You're going to be the best mother in the world, Lily. You have more patience than anyone and you have so much love inside of you. The girls are so lucky to have you for a mother."

"Momma, don't. Please" I spoke quietly, not wanting to upset her but not wanting to hear anymore of what she had to say.

"Lily, I know there are so many things you haven't forgiven me for and you don't need to forgive me. I don't deserve it. I just want you to know that no matter what, I love you and I'm so glad that you're my daughter."

"Momma, I appreciate that. I really do but right now, I just want to focus on my daughters and my husband. I've lived in Molly's shadow for so long and now is my time. She's gone and I'm still here. She can't come back, she can't give us the opportunity to save her. She didn't want saving. I tried. I tried so hard but she made her choice."

She nodded, holding back her tears. "Yes, Lily, she made her choice. Molly was troubled and you tried to help her when she turned her back on everyone else. You gave her everything she needed and she still chose to end her life. No one blames you. Please stop blaming yourself, Lily. It wasn't your fault."

I stood there and sobbed because it was everything I had needed to hear back then when it happened. She gave me everything I couldn't give myself that night but I still couldn't let it go. I still blamed myself and I hadn't even realized it.

My mother held me while I cried. I was hormonal and postpartum and my sister was dead. My babies bore her names. She'd been two totally different people and I gave my two little girls her names.

I could only pray that their lives would turn out happier than hers. Hers had ended in a grave far too soon. Theirs began in happiness and love. I promised them that I'd always give them that same love and happiness for the rest of my life.

I stayed there in my mother's embrace for a very long time that night. I needed it more than I'd realized. It was well after four am when we went back to bed. We hadn't talked. Not a single word. Nothing needed to be said then. We would get around to it eventually.

I was still sleeping when Jason left. I felt the kiss he gave me and smiled in my half asleep state. I hated that he had to leave so early but it had been an emotional night and I was tired.

I woke to the sunlight pouring into the room and sat up startled when I saw the clock. It read 11:00 and I jumped out of bed, racing down the hall to the nursery. I opened the door to find both girls napping and my mother sleeping in the soft recliner in the corner.

I laid a blanket over her, kissed my girls and took the opportunity to shower and have a cup of coffee before they needed to be fed again.

I was just beginning to warm their bottles when momma came in and sat her small suitcase in the foyer. I glanced over at her and frowned.

"It's time for me to go home and take care of your Daddy. I'll leave once Jason gets home. You guys have got a good handle on this. I'm just a phone call away if you need me."

"Thank you, Momma. For everything."

"You're welcome, Lily."

We spent the rest of the day just enjoying the babies and talking about things that didn't really matter all that much. It was the best way to spend our last day together for a while.

I was so grateful for her help and I told her so all day. She helped me prepare dinner while the girls took their afternoon nap. We made fried chicken, potatoes and veggies with homemade biscuits and gravy. Momma made her world famous lemonade and iced tea so that we had some when she left. She stayed for dinner and then gave Jason and I hugs and kisses and then she was gone.

For the first time ever we were alone with our twins.

Chapter Seven

The months went by way too quickly and soon the babies were teething and starting to crawl. We'd taken them to visit my parents many times and it broke my heart that Jason's folks had passed before they were able to meet our girls.

I knew it hurt him that he didn't have a family to celebrate the birth with. He was the last in his family remaining. He was an only child and the only one left. But now, now he had us and he said that was all he needed anyway.

Momma and Daddy treated him like he was their son and I loved them so much for that. They had a good relationship and he never complained about them. My husband and my father were good friends and went fishing together often. It made my heart all warm and fuzzy to know that they got along so well. I realized that I was lucky that they were close. Most families weren't but then our family wasn't most families.

For that I was grateful. I wouldn't trade our family for any other. We may have our problems but at the end of the day we loved one another and that was the important part of all of this.

The girls were growing so fast and I barely had time to shower these days but I wouldn't have wanted it any other way. I loved being a mother. No matter how tired I was at night, being mom to Molly and Daisy was the best part of every day. They challenged me and some days they drove me to near madness but they were beautiful and growing up too fast for my liking.

Tonight my parents were coming to baby sit so that Jason and I could have a date night. Momma was excited to spend the whole evening spoiling her grandbabies. I was happy to let her spend an evening with them. Watching the girls bond with my mother was just one more reason I loved being their mom.

Even as much as she loved them, I could see the pain in her eyes when she said Daisy's name. I worried that as they approached the age that Daisy was taken it would be too much for her. She still had a hard time when the anniversary came around. She denied it more and more as the years went on but we all worried for her then. She would withdraw for a few days and shut us all out.

I hoped this year, with the girls being here, she wouldn't shut herself off and would talk to one of us. Daddy had been trying for years. She'd always been this way he said, even when Molly was alive.

What happened with my sister nearly destroyed her. He told me about how strong she was every day in front of the cameras, with the police, with everyone, including him. It was when the doors closed at the end of the day, when she was all alone, that she fell apart. She collapsed into his arms and he held while she sobbed most of the night. She barely slept. She barely ate.

This went on for months, he said. He did everything to convince her that he didn't blame her. I didn't believe him so how could she? I wanted to ask him if he ever spent one minute blaming her because there were times when I did.

I didn't want to admit it but I did. She was there. She should have watched her. Who just puts a baby down and turns their back on them? How did she not hear him take her?

Yes, I blamed my mother for letting my sister being taken. She was the reason that Molly was abused. She was the reason that Molly existed. She was the reason that Molly was dead.

I said it. To myself. Never to her. Never to anyone. That wouldn't be kind and I was a kind person who never wanted to hurt my mother.

I hated that I felt this way. I hated that I blamed her. Rationally I knew that she didn't do anything wrong. She didn't plan for her daughter to be taken. She didn't plan for any of this. She'd done her best to pick up the pieces of their lives when Molly came home.

She was an amazing mother to Molly and to Daisy. She was an even better mother to me and I loved her so very much. She'd given us structure and rules. She also gave us the freedom to be ourselves and the ability to think for ourselves.

She was my mother and I loved her, but I blamed her. There was nothing that was going to change that.

And I hated myself every day for that.

Date night came and went, the holidays came and went. The girls grew and were so close to walking. Jason and I were thrilled with the thought of our babies being toddlers. We'd all finally settled into a routine and life was good.

Except.

Every time I took the girls out I panicked. I worried that someone would take them. I woke up screaming from nightmares about that very same thing. Jason worried that I was obsessing over something that wasn't going to happen.

I reminded him often how it had happened. It did happen. Children were taken. Children were abused. People did horrible things to little kids.

I knew this all too well. It had happened in my family. It had happened to my sister.

And it killed her.

If I was paranoid then I had every reason to be so.

Jason did his best to try to calm my fears about things that could happen to the girls. I appreciated him for it but I still hated taking both girls out by myself. I felt that I couldn't watch them both the way I needed to when I was alone.

I needed another set of eyes so I made him go with me on errands or I didn't go at all. I would order in the groceries or whatever it was that we needed. With Jason being the only one still working this put a lot of undue stress on him but I just couldn't. I couldn't take the risk of someone taking them.

I didn't want my girls to ever experience anything that had happened to my sister. So I stayed home and I ordered stuff for delivery.

Every weekend was filled with errands. The girls hated it. They hated their car seats. They hated the shopping carts and the noise and the people. They hated every part of it.

It was slowly dawning on me that I was raising them inside of a bubble and it wasn't healthy for them. This was not living and I knew it but those fears just hung between me and rational thought and the fears won every time.

Sooner or later I was going to have to let them out of my sight. I knew this. I really did but I couldn't fathom how that was going to happen. They were going to have to go to school.

Or I could homeschool them. I said it more than once to Jason.

"Damnit Lily, you're screwing them up. They're scared to even go outside to play. This isn't healthy for the girls or for you. You can't dwell on the danger of someone taking them. What happened to Molly was a one in a million chance."

"But it happened, Jason. Do you know what they did to her? No, you fucking don't. You don't know that they sold her to grown men. Men your age took my sister who was THREE years old and they fucked her. They used her body for their disgusting fantasies. They sold her to people to abuse her, beat her, rape her with inanimate objects. Should I keep going?"

"Stop it, Lily. I know that they hurt Molly. I understand that. I know it took her down a horrible path and that she was never the same. I'm sorry that happened to her. I'm sorry that you had to be the one that she leaned on but our girls aren't her. We have to let them live. They have to be able to go outside and live, Lily. They're babies and they don't even know what a park is. They've never been on a swing or a slide. You don't take them for walks or play outside with them. You've got them in this house like they are prisoners. They're not Molly. No one is going to kidnap them at the grocery store or the park."

"You don't know that. You can't know that, Jason."

"And you don't know that they will, but it's a chance we have to take so that they get to live a full life. They deserve to have friends and be happy. They will end up hating you if you keep this up. You're going to destroy our family, Lily. Think about it rationally."

I burst into tears. "I know you're right," I said between sobs. "I know that the chances of it happening is nearly impossible but it did happen to Molly and I'm scared. I'm scared that I'm going to wake up and realize that something has happened to one of them and I'll have to live this nightmare all over again."

"Baby, I won't let that happen. I won't, I swear."

He pulled me into his arms and he let me cry it out. He understood where my fear and craziness came from. He understood that trauma makes you do stupid things that make no sense because your brain processes it differently. And he loved me. This man loved me enough to put up with this side of me that he had to talk off the ledge. He'd been doing it since we'd started dating. I don't know what I would have done without him in my life. Jason kept me strong and held me up. He gave me love and space. He allowed me to feel things and he did his best to help me process all that had happened in my life.

He never patronized me. He never made me feel small or stupid. He helped me see past the fear, past the trauma of losing my sister the way I had. I loved him for all of that. He was the best man I'd ever known.

Hours passed before I could sit up and face him. I hated that I felt this way. I hated that he had to pick me up and keep me sane. I'd been in therapy. We'd been in therapy. He'd been there with me, trying to help me work through it all.

He reminded me that I was loved and I was safe with him. There wasn't anywhere else that I wanted to be. Without Jason, I'd be lost.

Chapter Eight

I lay back that night and thought back to when we'd first met, Jason and I. I'd been working at the diner for the summer and he'd just moved to Catskill. He walked in just as I was about to pour a cup of coffee for Earl, one of our regulars. The door hit my arm when he pushed it open too fast and I dropped the coffee pot. Thank God it was empty but I still had the scar on the top of my foot from where the glass was embedded in it.

He'd begged for my forgiveness and I rolled my eyes at him as I tried my best to pull the glass out of my foot.

"Stop trying to take that out. You need to go to the hospital. At least let me take you."

I shot Jason a look that said I'd rather shave my legs with a cheese grater than go with him to the emergency room.

"I'm not a killer or anything. This was just an accident. Things like this don't happen to me. Ever. I swear."

He was mumbling and speaking way too damn fast for anyone inside this diner. I only worked here because the townspeople gave great tips. They all had known me forever and never failed to tell me some funny little story about when I was a little girl. Hell, Earl had told me just this morning about the time I was just learning to walk and Momma took me to the store and I slipped on some water and crashed into the soup can display sending soup rolling down all the aisles.

But this guy, with his dark hair and blue green eyes, was just too much. I wanted to hate him since he'd caused me pain and ruined my day of tips but he seemed so genuinely sorry. I wanted to forgive him. In spite of my better judgment, I wanted to forgive him.

I finally gave in to the pain and him, and let him drive me to the emergency room. He insisted on staying with me until I was done so he could drive me home. I'd given up trying to fight him on anything about an hour into our wait to be seen. He sure could talk a lot.

Unfortunately, I found him fascinating and I hated myself for that. We'd already been waiting two hours and he hadn't stopped talking for more than one minute. I stood up to go to the restroom and he jumped to his feet.

"I just gotta pee, you don't have to go with me."

"But you can barely walk. I should probably carry you so you don't injure your foot more."

He immediately bent to try to scoop me up and carry me and I moved as fast as I could to get away from him.

"Stop moving."

"Stop trying to pick me up then."

"But you can't walk. You have glass in your foot. You could cut a tendon or something if you walk too much."

"That's a chance I'm willing to take. I have to pee and I'm certainly not going to let you carry me."

Jason stared at me in complete disbelief. It was like he didn't understand English all of a sudden. I wanted to hate him. I wanted to want him to leave me alone. I wanted to want to get away from him.

But I didn't. My heart kept skipping a beat every time he smiled at me with his lopsided smile. I hated that I thought he was the cutest boy I'd ever seen. God how I hated that.

I hobbled away from him and went to pee. I sat there even after I'd finished and wondered how less than three months after my sister died, this guy would wander into my life. This wasn't something I wanted or planned. I needed to stay away from him. He was trouble and I'd be damned if I was getting into trouble this summer.

Four hours and six stitches later, I was head over heels in love with Jason. I couldn't explain it, not even to myself.

Momma was worried it was too soon after Molly dying for me to be emotionally vulnerable. She thought I was replacing Molly with Jason. I'd told her that I wouldn't ever even think of trying to use Jason to get over my sister's death. I knew that I was grieving, that I needed time to face everything that had happened.

Jason was good for me though, he got me out of my head and back into the world. He forced me to be present and not dwelling on Molly's suicide. I hadn't told him about all of that yet. I didn't want to lose him yet. I wasn't sure he would be able to understand it all. I was terrified that he'd leave as soon as I told him that my sister took her own life.

Momma encouraged me to talk to him. She said I needed to let him know what had happened and why I needed time to myself. She was sure he was pressuring me into going out with him.

What I couldn't tell her was that I needed him to force me out of the house, to make me want to go out. He gave me hope that this feeling wasn't permanent. He gave me hope that somehow I would want to keep living.

I hoped that he'd be able to handle all that I would tell him someday about my sister. Maybe it wasn't my story to tell but he needed to know how I'd become the person that I was. Molly was a huge part of my life, even if she was gone now. I wanted him to know her. I wanted him to love her. She was my sister and my best friend.

Would he still like me? Would he still want to date me? I didn't know. I couldn't know without telling him.

I wanted to tell him. I wanted him to know everything about me. I wanted him to love me for everything that I was and for everything that had made me that way. I knew that I had to tell him.

And I would.

Soon.

⪼Chapter Nine⪻

Soon came a lot sooner than I'd anticipated. He picked me up and stopped less than a mile down the road. He shifted in his seat and looked at me seriously.

"Something odd happened today. Someone told me that your sister just died."

I blinked, trying to figure out what to say while the breath was knocked out of me. I was struggling and he was just staring at me waiting.

"Are you going to speak? Is it true?"

"Y..ye..yes." I stammered

"Why didn't you tell me?"

"I don't know. I just couldn't. I wasn't ready."

"How long has it been?"

""Three months, I think."

"That isn't a long time, Lily."

"No, it isn't. I'm pretty well aware of that, Jason. She was my sister. It hasn't been long."

"How are you doing?"

"I'm fine. I'm okay, I think."

He stared at me like he didn't believe me. I wasn't really sure that I believed me either.

"Jason, I don't want to talk about this right now." I spoke quietly, hoping he'd let it go.

"Have you talked about it with anyone yet?"

"No."

"Then you're going to talk to me about it. You gotta talk to someone, Lily."

"And if I'm not ready to talk about her with you?"

"It's been three months," he argued.

"Fine. What do you want to know?"

"She died."

"How?"

"She killed herself."

He sat in silence for a long while, letting it sink in. He looked at me with pity in his eyes, which was exactly what I was trying to avoid.

"I'm sorry. I'm really sorry."

"Don't you want to know how she did it? Everyone else does."

"No, not unless you want to tell me. I'm truly sorry, Lily. I didn't know."

"How could you know? You just moved here. You missed out on all the drama. Hell she didn't even live here. This town sure can talk though."

"All I heard was that she died. No one said she killed herself. I swear."

"It doesn't matter. She had a rough life. From the beginning."

"Do you want to tell me about her?"

"About Molly? Or Daisy?"

"I have no idea what that even means, but if you want to talk about them, I'm ready to listen."

I started to ramble almost immediately. "She was Daisy until she was three years old. Then she was abducted and Molly took over. Her therapist said it was to protect Daisy. The people who took her did horrible and awful things to her. Sexual things that no one should ever do to a child. She was just a baby. They did awful things to her. She was nine when they found her and brought her home. They were rescuing her while my mom was in labor with me. Weird huh?"

"So the day you were born, your sister who had been kidnapped came home? That had to be a hard time for your mother."

"Yeah, I guess. She never really said. All she ever said was that she was so happy that Molly came home and that she had both of her girls under one roof."

"Did you never ask her?"

"No, it never crossed my mind."

"Maybe you should. I'm sure it was hard on her."

"I guess. It was really hard on Molly. I do know that. She struggled with daily life type of things. She fought to be normal. She had to go to therapy so often. I grew up hearing her wake up screaming every night from the nightmares. Momma would always go in and sit with her until she went back to sleep."

"That must have been hard on all of you. How did your father handle things?"

I thought about that for a very long time before I answered. "He was strong and stoic as always. Daddy never let us see his emotions or if he even had any back then."

"Back then?"

"Yeah, he's different now. Molly's death really affected him. Now he makes a point of letting us know how he is feeling about things. But back then…he took care of us but he never let me or Molly see if he was sad or angry. We heard him and Momma argue from time to time but they didn't yell or raise their voice for any reason. I think that they thought that Molly would have a bad reaction to it."

"And did she?"

"Have bad reactions to things? Yeah, she did. More than once. Molly could be violent. Molly could lose it at the slightest inconvenience but it wasn't her fault. She'd been through a lot."

"Do you always do that? Make excuses for her bad behavior?"

"I'm not making excuses for her. My sister was abducted and abused physically, sexually, emotionally, and mentally. She had every right to act out."

"Did she? Or did she use that to her advantage to avoid accepting the consequences of her actions?"

"Why are you doing that?"

"Doing what, Lily?" he asked, looking at me curiously.

"Saying that she wasn't entitled to act out after all she'd been through?"

He shook his head and looked me in the eye, speaking quietly. "Lily, think about it. She was manipulating everyone. Maybe it really wasn't her fault or maybe she'd been taught to manipulate people to get what she needed or wanted? They taught her how to get what they wanted from those who did those things to her. Yes, she was abused. Yes, they did horrible things to her and she didn't deserve any of it. She may not even know that she's manipulating your parents and you. In fact, I don't think she does know. I think that in her life, she had to survive any way that she could. It must have been a hard life for her. It must still be hard for her."

I stared at him in disbelief. I tried to understand where he was coming from. He didn't know my sister, he had never met her. How could he judge her or anything that she'd been through? He wasn't being fair to her. He wasn't being fair to any of us. I didn't even know how to respond to anything he was saying. And yet, here I was still in love with him. I was listening to him, trying to see his point of view about Molly.

"I'm sorry, Lily. I really didn't mean to go on and on with my thoughts. Your sister is none of my business. I was just worried that maybe you weren't emotionally ready to be dating and I don't want to hurt you. I really, really like you, Lily. I more than like you. I just don't want you to start this and realize that you aren't ready. I don't think that my heart could take it."

I lifted my eyes to look directly at him and smiled. "I more than like you too. I'll admit that this isn't the best timing for any of this but I'm not stupid enough to not enjoy what the Universe has given me. There are going to be times when we don't agree on things. I don't want us to let those times ruin anything that may happen to us."

"Good. I really am sorry. I didn't mean to upset you or butt in."

"It's fine. It really is. People have always had a lot to say about my sister and how my family handled the whole situation. You didn't know her. She was amazing when she wasn't spiraling out of control. So, not all that often I guess." I shrugged and tried to laugh.

"You don't have to explain anything to me. I was out of place even talking to you about her. I was just worried that you might not be okay."

I could tell by the look on his face that he really meant that. Jason had such a kind nature about him. I reached out and took his hand, because I wanted to touch him. I wanted to more than touch him but I sure wasn't ready to tell him that.

He smiled at me and it warmed my heart. I loved the way he smiled. I loved the way he looked at me. How was I going to get through this day without blurting out that I was in love with him? It hadn't been nearly long enough for me to respectfully feel this way.

But respectability could kiss my ass. I wanted to kiss this man. I wanted to spend the night, making love to him until we were both spent, and then wake up with him in the morning to do it all over again. I pushed that thought out of my mind. I wasn't even sure where it had come from. Maybe it was because my sister had died recently. Or maybe it was because Jason was beautiful and I wanted to know everything about him.

And right then, as I was thinking about all of that, he leaned in and kissed me.

Chapter Ten

It was my first kiss. The very first kiss that I'd had as a grown up. Well, as a teenager close to being a grown up. I was thrilled that it was with Jason. He let the kiss linger, his hands in my hair pulling me closer to him. It was everything I'd ever dreamed of.
His lips were soft and tasted like cherry chapstick. For the rest of my life, I would love cherry chapstick. I had no idea if I was kissing him correctly. I just knew that I was enjoying every second of that kiss.

When he finally broke the kiss, I felt like the world had ended and I was lost and alone. He ran his thumb over my bottom lip and I smiled up at him.

"Sorry, I just couldn't spend one more second not knowing what you tasted like. How in the hell am I already in love with you, Lily?"

My heart skipped a beat and I felt the blush creep its way across my face. It was everything I wanted right now. I wanted him to love me. I wanted him to want to love me. This man, he was everything I ever wanted.

Who knew you could find your soulmate at 16 years old?

"Did I scare you? I'm sorry. It just felt right."

"Oh God, no. You didn't scare me, Jason. Why would you think that?"

"Because I just told you that I'm in love with you and you didn't say a word."

"I'm in love with you too. Are you insane? Of course I'm in love with you too. I just, well, I just can't believe that you feel the same way that I do."

"Why not? You're beautiful, Lily. If I could marry you today I would"

"I'm only 16, Jason. I can't marry you right now."

He laughed and pulled me in for another kiss. We spent the next hour kissing and touching one another in his car. If we didn't stop things were going to go too far and I wasn't ready for that just yet. As much as I wanted to sleep with him, I wasn't ready to do that yet.

I was still a virgin and for the first time ever I was ashamed of that.

I thought about Molly in that moment. I thought about how she had slept with so many men and I wondered why she felt the need to do that. Had she loved any of them, other than London? Or had she just been conditioned to believe that her body was nothing more than a plaything for men? Was she trying to feel something, anything, when she slept with them?

Why was I thinking of Molly while my boyfriend was kissing me? What the hell was wrong with me?

The night came to an end far too early and I sat outside my house, kissing him again. I'd have to go in soon or I'd be late for curfew and then Daddy would ground me. And I couldn't risk not being able to see Jason.

With one last kiss, I opened the door and ran for the porch, letting myself in without looking back. If I'd looked back, I'd have gone back to his truck and we would have been married by morning.

I kept walking straight to the kitchen where I grabbed a bottle of water and hurried to my room. I wanted to write down every single detail about this night in my diary so that I never forgot it.

This was a night to remember. It was also the first happy entry since Molly died and my heart was pounding remembering how amazing the kiss was. I couldn't wait to see him again.

I fell asleep that night, happy and smiling. I woke up the same way. He loved me. This beautiful boy loved me. Me, Lily Anders. He loved me.

And I loved him.

Jason and I had never been apart since that night. He became a fixture in my home. He was invited to all family events and holidays. My parents liked him. They said he was respectful and that if they could have handpicked a boy for me it would have been Jason.

He had charmed my mother, bringing her flowers and telling her that he saw where I got my looks from. He bonded with my father over fishing and baseball. They had even planned a fishing trip after the first time they met.

I was happier than ever and Jason was a great distraction from my sister dying. He kept me smiling all the time just by being himself. He was amazing, smart and handsome.

And I sound like one of those stupid girls who is all caught up in their boyfriend and forget everything and everyone else. I hated those girls. I couldn't be one of those girls.

But, Jason was one of those boys that made me one of those girls. We talked about Molly all the time. He made a point to learn as much about her as he could. He said that because she meant so much to me, he wanted to know her and see why I loved her so much. I wasn't sure that he would love her.

I wanted him to love her as much as I did but he didn't know her the way I did. And he never would.

Jason was someone I wanted to spend the rest of my life with. I know that seems crazy at 16 years old but when it's right you, you just know it.

We spent every minute we could together. We studied for exams together, for the SATs together and he helped me with my math because numbers just made no sense to me. He even helped me bring my score up by 40 points in Algebra. I helped him in English because his mind was more analytical than creative.

We were a true partnership from the very beginning. He introduced me to his aunt and uncle who had taken him in when his parents died the year before. He'd experienced loss too and it showed in his eyes when he showed me a photo of his parents. It was of the three of them and you could tell how close they'd been.

He'd lost them in a car accident, I'd learn. A drunk driver had crossed the double yellow line and plowed right into them. He still had a lot of emotions buried inside from having to live through the trial and relive the accident over and over.

That pain reminded me of how Molly had testified against her abductors. It wasn't exactly the same but having to relive it had been Hell on my sister so I could only imagine what Jason had felt having to hear how his parents died. He had to see the photos of the accident. He said that he had to sit there, he had to know how they'd gone.

He told me all about the trial and how he'd asked the judge to not sentence the man who'd killed his parents to death. He'd told the court that enough death had already occurred and taking this man's life wouldn't bring his family back.

I knew at that moment that Jason was a good man, no, a great man. He was selfless and thought of others feelings. I swore that night that I'd do everything in my power to make him happy in this life. I knew that someday we would be married and have a family of our own and perhaps in some small way, his parents would see him with his children, happy and content in his life.

Together we would be happy, in spite of all of the reasons we had to be sad.

⋝Chapter Eleven⋜

Jason and I remained inseparable until we graduated. He joined the military and for the first time in years, I had to say goodbye to him, not knowing when I'd see him again for sure. He shipped out to basic training four days after graduation and Momma held my hand as I cried, waving to him as he boarded the bus that was taking him away from me.

I spent a week crying because I missed him so much. One morning, Daddy came into my room and sat down beside me.

"Time to get up and live, Lily girl." He sounded so matter of fact when he'd said it that I nodded, not really knowing what to expect next.

He got up without another word, closed the door behind him and left for work. I stared at the back of my door for several long minutes then got up, showered, put on a skirt, nice blouse, and some sandals and headed for the kitchen.

Momma was pouring me a cup of coffee as I sat down. I took a sip of the heavenly liquid and smiled. It had long been established that coffee was my life's blood and I needed it just like I needed air to survive. Momma sat a plate in front of me with a donut then took a seat across from me.

"You look very nice today. Special occasion?" she asked before taking a bite of her own donut.

She was dressed in her normal black dress pants, white collared blouse and apron that said Penny's Diner across the chest. She'd been waiting tables there since I was just a little girl. Daddy had wanted her to give it up many years ago but she'd refused, saying that she'd have nothing to do if she wasn't at the diner.

"I'm going to find a job." She shot me a look that said she was thinking about college, not work, but she remained silent. "Just for the summer, Momma. I want to save some money so I don't have to work first semester."

She smiled brightly and nodded. "Such a smart girl you are my Lily bug."

Momma hadn't called me that in a very, very long time. It had been her pet name for me my entire childhood but once Molly had died, she hadn't called me that. My heart swelled with love for the woman who had given me life. Her life hadn't been easy after Molly was taken. She'd blamed herself.

I wanted her to be proud of me, to be able to tell her friends that her daughter was successful instead of them always asking about Molly. She deserved a break, to rest, to not have to answer all of those stupid questions the nosey ladies in this small ass town asked her daily.

I agreed with Daddy about her quitting the diner. She didn't need to be on her feet all day catering to people like she did. Penny always said Momma was the hardest worker she had and I didn't doubt it for one minute. Momma worked until just before Daddy got home, then she rushed home to make dinner, clean the house, and prepare for the next day.

Having her for a mother had been hard at times, but she always showed us that she loved us. She never missed a school event or any sports event that we'd have. Molly hadn't done much in extracurricular activities but I'd been quite active for most of my life. I'd taken ballet, played softball and basketball, was a cheerleader, was in French Club, FBLA, and Drama Club. I think I spent so much time at school or playing sports because I was avoiding being at home with Molly.

Not that I didn't love my sister, but most days it was very hard to live with her. She was moody and temperamental and I just wanted to be somewhere else. It helped Momma too because she got to get out of the house too. She caught the brunt of Molly's anger. Teenage angst mixed with mental health issues did not a nice child make. Molly was forever slamming doors and screaming that she hated my mother.

One night, she'd woken me up with her screaming and cursing and I stormed out of my room in my pjs and told her very bluntly that I wished she had never come home. I meant it then. I hated her when she was like that and I wanted her to go away. I screamed at her over and over again that I wished she'd died or just never came home. I screamed that she was mean to Momma and that she shouldn't have come back if she was just going to be mean.

Daddy had scooped me up and carried me out of the house. I was still screaming when he sat me in the truck, backed it out of the driveway and drove away from our house. I was immediately silent, not sure what was happening and more than a little scared that he was going to take me somewhere and leave me because I had been mean to Molly. They always took Molly's side because she was the one who got taken.

He pulled into the local McDonald's, pulled up to the drive through and ordered two chocolate milkshakes and paid for them. He handed one to me and took a long drink of his before he spoke. He'd parked in the parking lot under a light and turned to face me.

"Lily, I know that sometimes it's very hard to live with Molly. But we have to understand that she doesn't always mean everything that she says. She's not like you, Lily. She was hurt very badly and she needs you to help her understand that we love her and that she's safe with us. Do you understand?"

I nodded at him, then spoke, still holding my milkshake. "But Daddy, she's been home a long time now. Shouldn't she know that Momma is nice by now?"

"Yes, she should, Lily girl. Yes, she should."

He didn't say anything else for a while. We just sat there, late at night, in the McDonald's parking lot drinking our milkshakes. Momma would have told us both that we were going to have belly aches in the morning. She wouldn't approve of this but I didn't care. I got to sit in the truck with Daddy and have a milkshake.

Once we were done, Daddy drove home and parked in the drive. "Lily, I'm sorry that this has been hard for you. You're a very good sister to Molly and she does love you. She just doesn't know how to show love properly. It's not all her fault."

"Okay, Daddy," I said, rubbing my tired eyes. I was ready to get back in my bed and hug my teddy tight to me and go to bed. Morning was going to come very early I was sure.

The next day Momma didn't wake me for school. She didn't go to work either. Daddy was home too. That was the first time I really remember Molly being taken to the hospital. Momma went with her and stayed most of the day. Daddy stayed home with me and tried to make it as normal a day as possible. Right around lunch time I looked up at him and asked the question I'd been dwelling on all day.

"Is Molly gonna be okay?"

I was scared. I was scared that she wasn't going to come home. I was scared that she was mad at me for what I'd said the night before. I was scared that Momma hated me for saying I wished Molly had died. I was just a little girl and I didn't quite understand things that were going on around me. I sure didn't understand what was happening with Molly.

He answered me honestly. "I don't know Lily girl. I sure hope so. Right now, she's in the best place to get the help she needs."
"Okay, Daddy." It seemed to be the only thing I could say.

He came around the table and gave me a huge hug, holding me a little longer than normal. I was grateful for that hug then. Daddy was the only one who understood how much reassurance I needed.

"Lily, don't worry about Molly. Momma and I are going to take care of her and get her all the help she needs. We will worry about her. That's what Momma's and Daddy's do. Molly has been through a lot for being such a little girl and she just needs some help that we can't give her."

I listened carefully, trying to take it all in. I was too young to really understand it all. At that point, I still had no clue that she'd been kidnapped. She had always been a part of my life since she'd come back the day I was born. It would be a few more years before I understood that my sister had been taken and abused.

Daddy and I spend the day playing games and reading books. He made grilled cheese and tomato soup for lunch and ordered a pizza for dinner. Momma would be mad at him for sure. She would never have let me eat any of that together in one day only. I worried about Daddy being punished. Momma would be so mad that she would probably ground him from going fishing.

The next morning, Momma was in her normal place at the kitchen table. Daddy had gone to work early that morning since he'd have to take the day before off. Seeing me, she jumped up and grabbed a pop tart for me for breakfast. I instantly wondered what was wrong. Momma never let me have pop tarts on a school day.

"Take your time, Lily. I thought maybe you could stay home with me today."

I nodded and took another bite of my strawberry pop tart and drank my chocolate milk. Two days without having to go to school was almost too much for me. I liked school and I never knew Momma would let me miss school unless I was sick. Even then she watched me so closely that the moment my fever broke she'd be getting my school clothes ready for the next day.

Momma was forever going on and on about how important school was. She didn't need to try to convince me to go though. I really did like school. Learning new things was fun for me. School was the one place that Molly couldn't be the center of attention and I got to be seen and heard.

Momma was quiet while cleaning up the kitchen but I ran when she told me to go to my room and get dressed to go out. I had no idea what she had planned but I knew to go when she said go.

I quickly dressed in my jeans and favorite tee that had a glittery unicorn on it. It was purple and had long sleeves and I loved it. I decided to wear my pink Keds and green socks. I was sure that Momma would make me go change when I bounded back into the kitchen but she smiled at me and told me that I looked nice.

She was dressed in jeans and tee herself and I was shocked. I don't think I ever saw my mother wear jeans except for that day. She grabbed her purse and our jackets and we headed out the door. Once we were in the car she tuned the radio to a local pop station that played my favorite music. I was so shocked that I sat in silence, tapping my foot quietly on the floorboard.

She stopped when we got to the park and motioned for me to get out of the car. I thought for sure that she was going to take a seat on a bench while I played but she didn't. She led us down a trail I'd never been on before because I wasn't allowed to hike by myself.

We walked for a little while before she stopped and sat down on a log and began to cry. I stood there for a long time watching her. I finally took a seat next to her and wrapped my arms around her shoulders and rested my head there.

I hated to see her cry and I had no idea how to help her. I didn't know what was wrong but I knew that hugs always helped me when I was sad. She hugged me back but continued to cry.

"I'm sorry Lily. I wanted this to be a good day for you."

"It's okay Momma."

"You've just always gone with the flow and I'm so glad you're you, Lily. You're a very good kid, you know."

"Thank you," I said, not really sure what she meant.

"I know that your father and I sometimes forget that you need us just as much as Molly does. It's just, she's more demanding and you're, well, you're just a quiet little girl."

I nodded, but I really didn't know what she was going on and on about. She wasn't crying anymore and that's all I cared about. I wanted to keep hiking but it didn't seem that my mother was ready to move yet. She just sat there looking at me and wiping her face.

When she finally got up she started heading back towards the car. I thought she was going to take us home but she pulled into McDonalds and ordered me a happy meal and herself a salad. We sat at a table in the back and ate in silence.

I was happily munching on my fries when she started talking again.

"I wanted you to know that Molly is okay. She just needs to rest for a little while at the hospital. Unfortunately, you can't visit her for now. She's going to be fine. She just needs a little help to process some of the things that happened to her. I'm sorry if it scared you when she did what she did, Lily. You don't have to be afraid of her. She isn't going to hurt you or your father or myself. Hopefully she won't want to hurt herself anymore either."

I kept eating my french fries, looking down at the table while she rambled on.
"Molly is really a good girl. She didn't mean to try to hurt anyone. She was upset and that led to her melt down. She's been through so much. There is so much you don't know about her, Lily. Someday you'll understand."

I don't know what she was trying to accomplish. Maybe she wanted me to feel better about it all but all she'd managed to do was make me feel like she loved Molly more than she loved me.

Chapter Twelve

It was a few years later that I realized that maybe she didn't love Molly more than me. It was more that Molly needed her to focus on her more. I could handle my day to day life and I didn't need someone to constantly tell me that I was safe.

Molly did.

I could survive a trip outside by myself and never worry that someone was going to steal me and do awful things to me.

Molly did.

I could go to school and not fight with anyone. I could do my homework without being told a hundred times or sit at the table late into the night until I ate my dinner. I never, ever worried that I was going to be hit or beat or worse because I was upset and cried.

Molly did.

Nothing that I did frightened me. I didn't think Daddy was going to hurt me or that Momma was going to forget me.

I never worried that I wasn't good enough. I never worried that I wouldn't get to eat every day. I had no idea what it was like to survive in disgusting situations or be forced to do things that scared me or hurt me.

Molly did.

This would become the narrative of my very existence for far too many years.

Chapter Thirteen

I'm sorry if it seems that I resented my sister. There were days, weeks, months, you get the idea, that I did. Loving Molly wasn't the easiest thing. She didn't make it easy either. Rationally I knew that she really didn't deserve anything that had happened to her. Realistically I knew that she could have taken therapy more seriously and worked harder to be okay. Maybe it would have all turned out the same way, but she could have tried harder.

Molly was her own worst enemy. She wanted to be better but she didn't want to do the work. She wanted it to be easy. She wanted it all handed to her. She believed that Momma and Daddy could fix her. She believed that they were the ones who needed to do the work for her.

I loved my sister and I was the one who was there for her more than anyone in the last few years of her life. She was my best friend and I loved her more than anyone else in her life. She told me things that she never told a soul and I was so thankful that I knew her.

The real her.

I knew both Molly Anders and Daisy Anders and I loved them both.

I wish others had had that chance. I wish that they had seen her in the ways that I saw her. I wish they knew her the way I knew her. Molly was tough on the outside but inside, where it really mattered, she was fragile. She was a hurt soul. She wanted to be loved but was absolutely terrified of it.

When she'd met London, her life changed for the better. For a little bit of time, she was happy. I saw her smile. I heard her laugh. She talked about being in love and was making plans for the future. It was the first time she'd ever done that. Made plans for the future.

It was the life that I'd wished for her. It was the life that Molly deserved. She'd had so much taken from her and for once, someone had given her something back.

London truly loved her. He wanted to help her, to give her a reason to live. I wish it had worked. He was so devastated when Molly died. He'd made plans for their life together. He'd planned out the next 50 years. London knew that they'd have 2 children, that they would marry in my parents' backyard, Molly in white, him in black. They would dance to Endless Love, because he knew that they were soulmates and their love knew no end.

His world crashed down around him the night I had to tell him she was gone. I don't think he ever believed that she'd do it. I knew darn well that she'd told him about the demons she fought daily. Hell, they'd met because he'd found her passed out in the street.

Molly had told me once that she'd fallen in love with him the moment she looked into his eyes. She said she saw her future in them. I had wanted to believe her so badly.

I wanted to.

I didn't. Not for one second. Molly had attempted to take her own life more than once and there was no way that I believed that she wouldn't try again. There was going to come a day when she'd succeed and London would never forgive her or himself.

I could see how much he loved her. When he learned that she had Dissociative Identity Disorder, he never wavered. He learned everything he could about DID and did his absolute best to help Daisy when she was the one in control. The problem was, Daisy was a lesbian and she had no recollection of London or his life with Molly.
Daisy had a girlfriend, Emma-Lee. Emma-Lee was kind and loved Daisy but handling her DID wasn't something she was capable of doing. Molly even went so far as to pretend she was Daisy to spare Emma-Lee the trauma of knowing her girlfriend wasn't around all that much.

It became too much for Molly though as she fell deeper into love with London. She smiled a lot during that time. She seemed genuinely happy and I think, for a brief moment in time, she was. He helped her heal a little. He helped her forget that she was a victim and allowed her to just live inside of his love.

He protected her from the world outside that judged her. He never let a soul disrespect her, including herself. London really loved my sister.

But as much as he loved her, I don't think he was prepared for what came with loving Molly. She was determined to find others like her, others who had been hurt by Jim and Diane. She'd gone so far as to tell momma that she wanted to see Jim.

My parents both knew this was a bad idea. They knew he would manipulate her and try to destroy her. They did, however, support her in her decision to find the others. They understood that she needed them. They were her family. They all had the same pain burnt into their souls.

London couldn't understand why she clung to these people the way that she did. He felt that she needed to focus on those of us that were here, in the same state, in her life day to day. What he would never understand was that she felt more at home with those people than she did with us.

Not that it was a competition or anything but this is just how the reality of the situation was. Molly needed them to feel like she was like someone else. She needed someone else out in the world who understood what she'd gone through, and she needed to see them surviving every day.

That's the part I think that mattered the most and yet went unfulfilled. Her connection to them was undeniable. The biggest problem was that most of them had figured out how to move past all of the trauma and spent hours upon hours working with therapists and doctors and their own families to move past it and put it behind them. Molly didn't. She never would.

Because doing so would mean that she'd have to admit that something was wrong and she couldn't fix it by herself. Molly was the protector. Molly was the strong one, the one who kept Daisy safe. She was the one who held on when there wasn't a reason to hold on anymore. She was the one who never faltered.

Oh my God. Molly wasn't the one who took her own life. Daisy did it. Daisy decided to end it all.

How had no one ever thought of that before? Here we all thought that Molly had made the choice to leave because Molly was the one we all gravitated towards. Molly was the one we relied on to protect Daisy from the truth. Molly was the one we trusted would be okay at the end of the day. We had all blamed Molly.

I raced to my bedroom to find the note. I'd kept it all these years. It had mattered, her last words. London hadn't wanted me to have it but he'd given it to me in the end. I think it was his way of letting her go, forgiving her in a sense.

I unfolded it and reread those words. It all made sense now.

"Some people think that when you kill yourself that the whole world will realize what a tragically beautiful soul you were. I don't believe that. Suicide isn't something to glorify. It's a way out for those who can't find peace with what has happened to us. The funny thing is, so many of us are desperately seeking forgiveness for something that we thought we did or for something that never really existed anywhere but in our minds. I'd forgiven Amy and Scott. I'd even found a way to forgive Jim and Diane with my mother's help. She forced me to see that without that forgiveness I would never be able to heal. What she forgot to tell me was to forgive myself. I've hurt so many people but most of all I destroyed myself.

I did my best to put Molly aside and live Daisy's life but the more I tried, the worse it became. It took me a really long time and a lot of therapy to understand that I was and am Molly. Daisy died the day that Diane walked her out of that Wal-Mart. No Code Adam would ever bring her back.

Daisy never lived through my nightmares. She got to live free of the memories of what happened to me and I hated her for that. She didn't want the memories and I was forced to live with them.

I protected her and wanted her to come home to you all. I'm sorry that she never had the chance to live the life you thought she deserved.

I'm sorry. I know you're all in pain and you don't understand. I won't even pretend that I can explain it. All I can say is that when you live with demons, sometimes they win. I'm sorry. It's all I have. I know that it doesn't make this any easier on any of you, especially Amy, Scott and Lily. If I could take the pain away from you, I would. I don't expect you to understand. All I know is that I couldn't keep living a life that wasn't mine.

London, please know that I love you and that you were the one bright spot in a world filled with scars and monsters. I was so looking forward to being the wife you wanted me to be. I'm sorry. I'm so sorry.

They say that forgiveness is an act of love.

Please.

Forgive me.

Molly."

They were her words. They belonged to Molly but it wasn't her saying goodbye. This was her way of letting us know that she didn't want to end it. She was telling us that it was Daisy who did this. Daisy wanted to die, not Molly. Molly had every reason to live. She'd survived the worst thing to ever happen to someone.

How had I not seen it then? How had I never put it together before today? It all made sense now. Molly wanted to live. She wanted to marry London and have a life filled with love and happiness.

How did Daisy find out? That had to be what triggered this all. Daisy must have known that something happened. Had she remembered those days when she was gone? Did she understand all that had happened to her? Is that what sent her over the edge?

I wanted to tell Momma. I wanted her to know that Molly hadn't wanted to die. She had come to love Molly more than Daisy. We all had. Yes, Molly had her problems, but she admitted them and she constantly tried to find a better way. She failed nearly every single time but at least she tried.

Daisy didn't try. She let Molly take over. She let Molly live her life. The few times that she was in control, she fell in love with a girl and made a mess of her own life.

How had I not seen this? How had I not listened, really listened to what Molly said in this letter? How had London not known?

Had he not wanted to? Molly dying certainly made life easier for him and a lot of other people. God, I hated myself for thinking that. I hated that I was ready to accuse people of not loving her enough at the drop of a hat.

It was hard to love Molly. It was the hardest thing in the entire world but once you loved her, you loved her forever.

I hadn't really realized how much I missed her until this moment. I missed her laugh, the one that carried on the air around her. The one that made you wonder what was so funny and why you didn't get to be a part of the joke with her. I missed the way she'd call me on Sunday morning to ask me what was the name of the bagel place that I loved so much. I had always known that it was just an excuse for her to talk to me.

She'd always invite me to tag along for a bagel and coffee after too. I would give anything to get woken up on a Sunday morning and hear her voice on the other end of the phone one more time.

I missed my big sister, my best friend, the one person who had always loved me unconditionally. Most of my friends thought it was strange how much time I spent with her. I thought it was time worth spending.

Molly was smart, smarter than most people realized. Grades didn't mean everything and even though she brought home D's, Molly knew the stuff well. She held her own in grown up conversations about politics, religion, history, and current events happening in the world.

I'd been so proud of her then and I guess I still was proud of her. Death doesn't stop that. I was so mad at Daisy for taking my sister from me. I wanted to hate her for it but I couldn't. Daisy was childlike and innocent for the most part. Learning of what Jim and Diane had subjected her to had to be devastating.

I know Molly had been working with Dr. Morales on the integration of both personalities, but did that mean that Daisy found out? It was the only logical thing that could have happened to cause all of this.

A part of me wanted to call Momma and Daddy right away and tell them that Molly hadn't done it. That they had to stop blaming her because it wasn't true. The rational side of my brain forbid it explicitly.

Why open old wounds? Why have them lose them both all over again? That's what this felt like. It felt like hearing those words for the first time.

"Molly is gone.. It was suicide. No, not pills. She slit her wrists. I don't know, Amanda. I don't know."

I could still hear my mother's sobs as she talked to Aunt Amanda about my sister dying. It seemed like just seconds ago instead of years. They didn't know I was awake. They'd done their best to shield me from the awful truth of how she'd died.

I wasn't naive. I'd been around Molly and Daisy long enough to know that something like this was going to happen eventually. It still caught me off guard. She'd been doing so well at that time. London had been good for her.

Knowing how scared she must have been as it was happening haunted me. She was all alone, dying. What was she thinking? Did she regret it? Did she want to take it all back?

I wish I had gotten there earlier. I wish I'd been able to convince her to stay.

I hated myself for dwelling on this. Jason would be furious if he knew. He's told me time and time again that it wasn't my fault, nor was it my place to fix her life for her. She was a grown woman who'd been through Hell as a child. He was shocked she hadn't done it sooner.

I wanted to hate him for that. I wanted him to apologize but why? She wasn't here. And he was right. She had so many demons that she fought that she must have been so confused on which one was the worst.

I knew she had wanted to see Jim. I knew she wanted to confront him for all that he'd done to her. She believed that it would free her. When he died, she seemed so sad. I wanted her to be happy that he was gone. I wanted her to hate him but she was sad. Sad over a man that raped her and sold her. It made absolutely no sense to me.
When I started therapy my therapist told me that Molly had survivor's guilt and that sometimes people who had been taken and held for a long time began to love their captors. It wasn't unnatural for a child to care for the parent figure in their life. Most kids who were abused loved their parents even if they were horribly abusive.

I could never fully understand it because I hadn't lived with abuse. I had parents who loved me and cared for me. I hurt for every child like Molly.

When those others came to visit, I listened to their stories and some of them were awful. Jim had raped his own newborn daughter and later on he got her pregnant. What parent does that?

I thought of my girls upstairs sleeping and I knew beyond any shadow of any doubt that if Jason or anyone, tried to hurt them in any way, I'd kill them. No questions asked. No thought of human life being valuable. I would simply snap and kill them.

What scared me the most is that we lived in a world where kids like Molly were taken on a regular basis and trafficked. Too many times, no one was seriously looking for them. The police did their best but when there were no leads, like in my sister's case, they had no choice but to move on to another case they may actually be able to solve.

Molly was found by pure luck. Jim had done his due diligence to keep her out of the public eye. She was trafficked on the dark web before that was even a thing. My parents didn't know. Technology wasn't something they really fooled with at that time.

Now my mother had a cell phone and never left home without it. Back then she didn't even know what a computer was. She learned. Only because she began to understand that it could help her find Molly.

Daddy learned how to search the web too. They used it to get the word out about Molly. Not that it helped them but they did find others like them and were able to find help with all of the emotions and anger that they had.

Later my mother used it to find Dr. Morales for Molly. To think of my parents as early adopters of technology nearly made me laugh.

By the time I was old enough to walk and talk, computers were everywhere. They were household items that we all used every day. Now they were just a part of life we expected to be there when we needed it.

Molly had barely carried a cellphone much less owned a computer. She wasn't interested in what was happening online. She was too busy trying to avoid what was happening in her own life to care about anyone else's.

I didn't want to think about this anymore. I wanted it to all be over for good. Could that just happen already? Would I ever be free of my sister and her ghosts?

The anniversary of Molly's death was rapidly approaching. My mother always made a huge deal out of us all going to the cemetery together. Maybe she believed that we were all in the same place then. No matter what it was, I didn't want to go this year.

I'd just had twins less than a year prior. I wanted to stay home with my babies and be happy for a change. I'd cried enough over Molly and Daisy. I had no more tears left to shed for them.

I was tired and aggravated that my mother expected me to make an appearance. Jason had called her to let her know I wasn't feeling well. She told him to tell me to get my ass out of bed, into some warm clothes and get down to the cemetery.

She wasn't going to take NO for an answer so I might as well get it over with Jason and I settled the girls into their carseats, buckled them in, and started the long drive to her final resting place.

Momma had picked a beautiful spot that got sunlight about 80% of the day. Molly would have loved it. Daisy not so much. They were as different as night and day and it never ceased to amaze me that they both inhabited the same body.

I'd arrived with the babies and Jason in tow and my mother shot me a dirty look. She could be mad all she wanted but this was a family affair and Jason and my girls were family so they had every right to be here.

Of course she started everything with a prayer. It was my mother's way and you prayed whether you wanted to or not.

If you could leave and never turn around. Getting banned from our family wasn't a good idea no matter how you spun it. I wasn't in any mood to spin it either way.

I wanted to get this day over with so I could go home and pretend I was an only child again. Momma began her yearly talk about family and love beyond death. I'd heard of it since I was six so I was bored.

I often wondered what I would be like now if I'd grown up an only child. Would I be any different? Would I be spoiled? I longed to believe that I wouldn't be any of those things but reality was I probably would have. It was Molly who kept me grounded. She never let me forget that it could all be taken away in the blink of an eye.

I tuned in to hear my mother talking about when Molly had returned home and I instantly tuned out again. I glanced over at Jason who was doing his best to not regret sitting here instead at home watching football. I was more than a little pissed about that too for him. He worked hard all week and on the weekends he liked his manly football games.

I didn't mind them so much as it gave me time to read or crochet, or whatever it was I was into that week. We had twins and that didn't facilitate us having a lot of time to do any of the things we loved to do.

So having to give up our day to come to the cemetery was more than enough to make us both a little upset. Momma was droning on and on about Molly as a child, how she was so precious and sweet. Apparently we knew two totally different kids named Molly. She was none of those things. Not in the slightest. She lied and stole. She drank beer and smoked cigarettes. She beat me up and almost killed me.

None of those things were traits of a precious and sweet child. It was indicative of a child that had been abused for sure. Of course I'd forgiven her for those things years ago but listening to this at her grave was almost too much.

My mother remembered a child who didn't exist. She'd wanted that child to exist. She'd wanted Molly to be that kid. But she wasn't. She never could be. It wasn't who she was and Molly always stayed true to Molly.

Unless, of course, that she was Daisy. Then it was a whole different ball game.

Daisy was the complete opposite of Molly. Where Molly was loud, Daisy was quiet. Where Molly was in your face, Daisy stayed to herself and was shy. I didn't like Daisy. Not even a little bit.

Daisy was the kind of person that you just felt weird around because you could never get a read on them. I never could tell if she was happy to be around us, or if she just had no damn idea what was happening in her life.

In her defense, she wasn't out very often so I'm sure it was strange to have lost so much time every time she was around. I just didn't like her. It wasn't that she wasn't a sweet girl, because she was really sweet. It wasn't that she had annoying habits. Maybe it was because when she was out, Molly wasn't there.

Given the disease that she had I knew that that wasn't true, that Molly was always there. The problem I had with that is that she wasn't there. She had no idea what was happening with Daisy when Daisy was out. And she wouldn't find out unless someone told her. I couldn't be that someone. I didn't want to be caught in the middle of it.

Add it to the list of things I didn't want to be a part of with this family. Going to visit Molly today was another. I visited her on my terms. Today wasn't on those terms. It was on my mother's terms and she'd want to talk about how much Molly meant to our family. How they'd never stopped looking for her.

To be honest, I didn't need to be reminded that I wasn't the child that meant the most in this family. I just happened to be the kid that was left.

Chapter Fourteen

I hated that I felt that way. I hated that even with her in a grave, I still came second to Molly. She'd been the center of their world since she was taken and it had never changed. I used to wonder if it would be different had she never returned but I don't think it would have been any different. I would always be the kid that didn't get taken. What a horrible thing to be, right?

Jason tried to help me understand that it wasn't true, but he was wrong. It was true. I wasn't Lily, second daughter of Scott and Amy Anders. I was Lily, the one who didn't get taken or abused.

What a horrible way to see yourself. It wasn't who I wanted to be. I was just Lily. I was glad I didn't live through what Molly had. I wasn't sure that I would have survived it. I wasn't strong like Molly. I sure didn't want to live with the aftermath of it all.

I thought all about what Molly had lived through. Could I have done it? I don't think so.

Jason understood that it was irrational at times but he never made me feel that way. He always stood by me, protecting me. He knew me better than I knew myself at times. He knew what I needed before I needed it.

He was the one who helped me after Molly died. Before I met him, I was lost and alone. I didn't know who or what I was. I was just going through the motions of life. Then I met Jason and I could feel again. He helped me heal, helped me move past the anger and the fear.

He gave me the strength to be whole again. He continues to give me that strength and I am so thankful for him. We had our own family and for the first time in my entire life, I was first in that family. No one overshadowed me or needed things more than me. I loved Jason with my entire soul.

And yet, I still felt like that little girl who always came second when I was around my parents. Momma was the one who made me feel that way. Daddy did everything he could to make me feel loved. Momma needed to talk about Molly all the time. She still needed to be the mother of the child who was abducted. It was her entire identity.

She'd lived that life for so long that now that Molly was gone, she had nothing. She became nothing. It was sad to watch to be honest. I wanted her to find something else to be. I wanted her to want to be grandma to my girls, to love them, to spoil them. I was starting to believe that she would never be able to do that because she was so hung up on being Amy, Molly's mother.

It was hard to hate her for it. Boy had I tried. I wanted to hate her. I wanted to cut her out of my life. She may not have ever hit me, or hurt me physically, but she'd destroyed me nonetheless. I'd need a mother, someone who loved me. What I'd gotten was Molly's mother.

There were times I felt invisible in my own home. Molly needed so much of her time and attention. Molly needed help. Molly needed.

That was it. Molly. Needed.
Why hadn't I hated her? Why did her dying nearly destroy me? I should have hated her. I should have been happy she was gone and now I could be the only child. I wasn't any of those things. I missed my sister so much.

Jason understood that when no one else did. My friends worried that I was so sad over her death. They knew how hard it had been for me living in Molly's shadow. They'd wanted me to be happy. I loved them for that but they didn't understand.

They didn't know her the way I did. They hadn't loved her in spite of it all the way I had. I wanted them to understand why her dying was so bad. I couldn't explain it to them. There were no words that ever could. They would never understand the bond that Molly and I had had.

Some days I hated how much I missed her. Other days I knew that I missed her so much because we'd been so close and that that was important and special. It made no sense but as my therapist says, it was grief. Losing her had been my first huge loss.

In therapy I learned to allow myself to grieve for Molly. I had to feel the grief, cry the tears. I hated it. Grieving made me vulnerable and I'd vowed that I'd never be vulnerable. Vulnerable put you in positions like Molly had found herself in.

I was always aware of my surroundings. I was always aware of the people around me and how they were acting. I paid attention to little details that could identify anyone around me. I never sat with my back to a door. I never stopped scanning all around me no matter where I was. It was a habit I had formed out of necessity. I'd learned from what had happened to Molly.

I wasn't going to be a victim. I wasn't going to be caught unaware. I needed to know that I was in control. Once I'd met Jason I had started to relax some but I still remained vigilant. It was to be expected when your sister had been abducted. You never forgot that or moved past it.

It was just how it was when that was your life. People didn't understand it. Jason did. He learned all that he could to help me. He even went to therapy with me to learn how he could help me best. My therapist was impressed. I didn't tell her everything. No one knew everything, not even Jason.

I had lied to so many people for too long now and I wanted to tell someone but I couldn't. There was no way anyone would forgive me if they knew. I couldn't begin to know how to put into words what I'd done. Not that it really mattered. It was over now. It was done and I couldn't take it back.

I did what I had to do. I did what she'd asked of me. She was looking for permission to end it, to let go. It was the least that I could do for her. I'd watched her suffer for so long. I'd seen her downward spiral. She'd tried so hard to integrate but it wasn't working. She was lying to everyone.

Except me.
I knew the truth. I knew all of her truths. I was the one she trusted. I was sixteen years old. Not that that made it any better but I was young. I'd carried around her weight for so long. I'd seen her struggle for so long.

As much as London had changed her life, he hadn't made her better. He'd loved her and for that I'm eternally grateful, but he didn't make it easier for her. In fact, he made it harder. Molly fought harder to stay out so that she could stay with London. She held Daisy at bay and when Daisy did manage to come out, she pushed Molly further and further back. Molly struggled to regain control.

It scared me. Watching her fight between her personalities was scary to witness. Daisy had people who loved her and so did Molly. How could anyone decide between the two?

But it's what we were asked to do. Dr. Morales thought it would be good for Molly to know who people preferred. She thought it may help her with the integration. She was wrong. All it did was add stress to their lives. They were both worthy of being alive and having a life they could love.

Integration wasn't going to make that happen. It was going to take pieces of each and make them one but they'd lose things. Things that made them, them. How could you choose between them?

And if I had to choose, I would have chosen Molly every time.

Unfortunately I didn't get to choose. Daisy chose for us. She chose to lie to us all and let us believe that it was Molly who ended it all. I was so angry at her. I wished she was here so I could tell her.

But Daisy made sure that that would never happen.

Chapter Fifteen

Molly and Daisy's first birthday was fast approaching and Momma was getting worse. She insisted that we needed to have a princess party because that's what Daisy had had for her first birthday. Jason and I wanted a unicorn party for the girls.

Momma wasn't going to back down easy though. Jason decided that we were going to have unicorns and Momma could get over it. He had no idea the position he put me in with my mother. She wasn't going to go quietly that was for sure.

I ordered the unicorn decorations and cake and canceled the princess one Momma had ordered already. The lady at the bakery asked me at least twenty times if I was sure about canceling it. I lost my temper and told her to cancel it or she'd be wearing it and then the girls and I stormed out.

I just happened to storm out right into my mother. I was already fired up and I let her have it.

"Don't you dare think that you can decide what kind of first birthday party Molly and Daisy are going to have. I want a unicorn party and they are having a unicorn party whether you like it or not. I am so sick of having to walk on eggshells around you, Momma. The girls are MY children, not yours. They can't replace Molly. She's gone and there is no changing that. You still have me and if you stop acting like nothing else matters except Molly then mayne, just maybe, you'd have time to be a grandmother to the girls."

She stood in stunned silence as I stormed off, the girls still sleeping even though I'd been yelling very loudly. They stayed asleep the whole walk home and I was thankful for that. It gave me a chance to cool down before I got home to Jason. He was going to be so proud that I'd had an emotional outburst. I'm sure he thought I wasn't even capable of them.

By the time I got the girls out of their stroller and changed and into their bouncy seats, I'd calmed all the way down. I started to feel bad for the way I yelled at my mother. I was just about ready to call her and apologize when Jason came in and kissed me on the cheek.

"I hear you had an eventful day. Wanna tell me what happened?"

I shot him a dirty look over my shoulder and continued making the spaghetti sauce.

"It wasn't eventful. I ordered a cake."

"And?" He stood behind me, his hands on my waist.

"And my mother happened to show up."

"Is that all? She just happened to show up and you just happened to yell at her?"

"I did not yell at her. I spoke passionately about a subject that she needed clarification on."

"And did you clarify things?"

"Yes, I did." I said it matter of factly and continued with cooking dinner.

He laughed and kissed the top of my head then went to sit across the counter from me at the breakfast bar.

"I got an earful about it from your father. He didn't seem upset that you lost it on her, but he did seem angry that he had to deal with her after."

"Well, he married her, he should have to deal with her."

We both laughed and I held the spoon up for him to taste the sauce. After approving dramatically, we dropped the subject of my mother. With any luck she'd heard what I'd said. If not, I'm sure half the town would fill her in since apparently, I was the topic of conversation that evening over the dinner table.

Once dinner was done, we sat across from one another and I burst into laughter in the middle of eating.

"I totally yelled at my mother in the middle of the street today."

"You sure did, babe. I didn't think you had it in you."

We both laughed even more. I loved him more than ever for teasing me about this. The entire situation could have turned into a complete mess but he managed to keep me from falling apart thinking about what I'd done.

Momma wouldn't forgive me anytime soon but I didn't care. She'd be at the birthday party, there was no doubt about that. What I worried about was how she would treat me and the way she'd act when she was here. My mother could be very cold and she would shut you out very quickly.

Jason told me not to worry about her and what she'd do. He would handle it, but Jason hadn't spent a lifetime with her as his mother. I knew just how she could be when she didn't get her way.

My mother was a bit of a control freak. Daddy said she wasn't that way before Molly was taken. He said she had been very laid back and that's why he'd fallen in love with her. She had been a great mom to Daisy, spending every day teaching her and arranging for elaborate play dates for her. He talked about those days longingly.

I think he missed her even though they were still married. Their life had changed so much after Daisy was taken. They had to learn to rely on one another because they really couldn't trust anyone else. They had no clue who was a friend and who wasn't after that. They finally found some real friends after they joined the support groups but I can't imagine how hard it must have been to be a part of that group of people.

They'd all lost a child in some form. Some of them lost them to disease, some to kidnapping, some to murder, others to abuse. None of them were normal parents by any means. They'd all lost something important and there was no way to replace it.

I can't imagine my mother opening up to those people about what had happened to Daisy. Daddy said that they were lucky that they were able to find Daisy. It was something that they never thought would happen. They had remained hopeful of course but statistically they weren't going to find her alive.

I'd once overheard Daddy say that it may have been best if Jim had killed her. I hated that I agreed with him. I hated that Momma didn't.

This party wasn't going to be easy for me or for Momma. She loved the girls. I knew that. I appreciated that. What I didn't like was that she had to take over the party. This was my first time throwing a party for my daughters and I wanted to do it by myself.

I wanted to experience everything that came with being a mom. The girls were my whole world and I loved them so much. I only wanted to give them the best life possible. I wanted my mother to be a part of their life. They only had one set of grandparents and I wanted them involved in my girls' lives.

It wasn't only my fight with my mother that was going to make this party awkward and hard. I'd invited London and Molly, his daughter. He'd split from his wife recently and he'd called asking about the girls and before I could stop myself I invited him.

I didn't want him to feel left out of our lives because he'd loved my sister so much. I didn't want him to think that we didn't care for him, or remember how good he'd been for Molly. He didn't have much family around so he needed us and I did care for him.

Momma was going to be caught off guard to find him here, but it was my house and I could invite whomever I wanted. Jason had thought it was a great idea to have London over. He knew what it was like to be alone in the world so he was happy to welcome London into our home.

They had more in common than either of them thought and I couldn't wait for them to become fast friends. It would be good for them both to have someone who understood their plight in life.

The day of the party dawned bright and sunny. I spent the whole morning cleaning and putting together party favors for babies. Jason took care of the girls as I stressed over the party. He bathed them, fed them, and even dressed them for the party. He was husband and father of the year for sure this year.

As 3pm approached, the first guests arrived. I greeted them at the door and showed them into the great room where the party was all set up. The girls were awake and happy, toddling around in their beautiful dresses. They'd both started walking about a month before.

Molly took her steps first and Daisy got so mad about it she took her's just a few minutes later. They were the best of friends but also extremely competitive with one another. Daisy crawled first followed immediately by Molly. I could barely keep up with them both.

The house was full of kids laughing and crying when my mother walked in. She stopped dead in her tracks when she saw London holding Molly. His own Molly was sitting on the floor playing with Daisy.

I couldn't tell if she was mad or just shocked. She shot me a questioning look and I shrugged. I knew that she was going to ask a million questions later but for now, she continued on into the great room.

Once Momma and Daddy had arrived, the party went into full swing. Momma was in her element, picking up kids, giving hugs, kissing boo boos, and smiling at parents. She jumped into gear helping to make plates of food for the kids, changing diapers when someone needed it, and kept a very close eye on London, his wife, Laurie, and of course, Molly.

I watched her for a while, wondering what she must think about London having married and now being a father. She stopped a few times to help his Molly with her plate or to show her how a toy worked. For a brief moment, I saw the mother I'd always wanted her to be for me.

I looked up to find London at my side.

"She's good with kids," he said quietly, glancing over at me.

"Yeah, she is."

"Sort of wishing she'd been this way with you, aren't you?"

"How did you know?"

"Molly used to tell me that she wasn't very attentive towards you and that you got left out often. I think it really bothered her that she was the reason for that."

I looked up at him again, a frown on my face. "She worried about too many things that were out of her control, that sister of mine."

I walked away from him because if I had stayed, I would have lost it right then and there. I had to busy myself to keep from crying. I decided that cake would distract me enough and so I headed for the kitchen to find the lighter and candles.

Jason came up behind me, turned me to face him and pulled me in for a big hug.

"You don't always have to be strong, Lily. It's okay to still miss her and to be sad about the whole situation."

I let my tears fall for a few minutes before gathering myself and nodding at him. I stood on my tippy toes and kissed him.

"I love you, Jason. Thank you," I said, rummaging through the drawers looking for the candles.

"You're very welcome, babe." He began to open drawers and look for candles too. Within a few seconds we had found them and Jason got the cake out of the fridge and let it rest for a few moments. "Ready?"

I nodded, not trusting myself to speak and followed him out the door with the two smash cakes I'd ordered separately for the girls. Momma was gathering the kids around for cake and I appreciated her so much for helping right then. She'd never know what that meant that day.

The rest of the party flew by, the girls were covered in cake but they had the best time. We laughed and snapped a million pictures. Jason was there by my side the entire time, his hand on my lower back. I realized how lucky I was to have him as my husband and best friend.

Momma and Daddy stayed to help clean up and so did London and Laurie. Molly was happily playing with baby Molly and Daisy in their room. Jason had given them a shower already and put them in the pjs. Momma and I were in the kitchen putting food away when she asked what I'd been dreading.

"What's the deal with London, Lily?" She had her back to me, putting food away into the fridge.

"There's no deal with London, Momma."

"I didn't know that you'd stayed in touch with him. Your father and I had tried to do the same but he didn't seem interested. So, why is he here?"

"Jason and I ran into him a few weeks back and we just invited him and his family. I think Jason just wanted to have a tiny piece of Molly here for the girls, Momma. That's all. Nothing underhanded or evil happening here at all."

"I didn't say that, Lily. Why must you do this every time I try to talk to you?"

"You insinuated it, Momma. You always have some kind of problem with everything that I do. This was my girls' party and I invited someone that I wanted to celebrate with us. If you have a problem with that, that's your problem, Momma. London loved Molly and he was good for her. Did you ever think about how much it must have hurt him to see you and Daddy? Did you ever think about how he felt? Or was it about how you felt, as usual? You aren't the only one that lost her, Momma. And you sure as Hell aren't the only one that misses her. For the love of all things that are holy, the man named his daughter after her just to have a piece of her in his life. Maybe, just maybe, he was grieving and hurting and just didn't want to be reminded of how much he'd lost at every turn back then."

I stormed out of the kitchen, leaving my mother speechless in my wake. My rage grew when I realized how quiet the living room was, and how all eyes were on me. They'd heard it all. London was staring at me with complete admiration shining in his eyes.

Very few people had gotten the best of my mother and I had managed to do it in the middle of a house full of people. I felt bad that I'd embarrassed her, but she deserved everything I had said.

I was sick and tired of walking on eggshells because she lost a daughter. I lost a sister. London lost his girlfriend. She wasn't the only one hurting and she needed to know it. It was time for her to realize how selfish she was being.

I didn't want to hurt her. I knew she was hurting still. We all were. I reminded myself that she'd lost her twice.

After everyone left, I sank down into the couch and closed my eyes. I wanted to understand my mother more than anything. I tried to imagine what she had lived through but I couldn't. I don't know that I would have reacted the same way that she did. We were very different mothers.

I blamed her. She was the reason my sister was taken. She was the reason that Molly wasn't here anymore. Hell, she was the reason Molly even existed at all. Had she been a better mother, a more responsible mother, Daisy would never have been taken.

It was never supposed to happen. If she'd been watching her, Daisy would have grown up with our family. She wouldn't have been abused. She'd still be alive.

I hated my mother for what had happened to Molly.

Chapter Sixteen

It had been weeks since the girls' party and I hadn't spoken to my mother once. Jason had asked a few times if I was sure this is how I wanted this to play out. I reassured him that right now, I needed to take this break from her. I couldn't tell him how long the break was going to last because I had no idea myself.

Daddy called regularly to check up on the girls and I was pretty sure that Jason had spoken to my mother on more than one occasion. I knew that she loved the girls and they missed her.

They asked for their Mimi every day and I told Jason to take them to see her. There was no sense in hurting them because I was mad at her. The girls loved their grandmother and Jason obliged me and took them to see my parents.

He came home with food and tons of gifts for the girls. Momma was doing her best to stay away and give me the time I needed to sort through everything that was bothering me. Jason told me all about what had happened while he was there.

I only half listened to what he was saying. I listened to the parts about my children and Daddy. Jason went on and on about my mother.

"Can you stop?" I snapped.

"No, actually, I can't. You've let this go on too damn long now, babe. It's okay to be mad at her for what happened in the past. It is not okay to shut her out of your life. You've already lost Molly. Do you really want to lose your mother too? This is just a petty fight and you're acting silly."

"Silly? You're kidding me, right? She came into my house and questioned who I had invited here. She had the audacity to insinuate that London didn't belong here because he wasn't family. He's family to me."

"And you have every right to invite him here, and anywhere you want. He's your friend and I think you need him around. Both of you lost someone very special to you. He's a good guy, Lily. But, she's your mother. She loves you."

"She has a hell of a way of showing that. I've always been an afterthought in her life. Molly came first. No matter what. Did you know that she even forgot my birthday one year? How do you forget your daughter's birthday? Especially since I was born the night that Molly was found."

"I'm not saying she was a good mother. I'm not saying she was a good human being. What I'm saying is, haven't you both lost enough? Do you really want to never see her again?

Wouldn't you be heartbroken knowing that she passed away without you having spoken to her? No matter what has happened between the two of you, she is your mother, Lily."

" Can you stop? She's not dying, Jason. There is plenty of time to fix things later. I just want to be mad right now."

"Tomorrow isn't promised, babe. We both know that all too well. Don't be mad so long that you never have the chance to fix things. You may wake up one day and regret how long you held that grudge."

I sighed heavily. He was right and I hated that he was. I wasn't done with being angry at her yet. I needed a few more days, but if Molly's death had taught me anything it was that people could be gone in the blink of an eye. I didn't plan on staying angry with her forever, but I did plan on being angry for a long time.

Jason came and gave me a kiss and then went upstairs to leave me with my thoughts. And, I had a lot of them. I thought about all those years that I was invisible to my mother. It had been hard to be her child and realize that I didn't matter as much as Molly did. Part of me understood that she did love me and that Molly just needed her more. Now that I was a mother, I could see how she gave attention to the child who was hurting and needed her the most. I was pretty self-sufficient and didn't really need her in the same way.

I wasn't scarred or hurting. I wasn't lost or found. I just was.
And that was the problem because she saw me that way. She saw me as the daughter that didn't need her to hover or take care of her. I was the one she didn't have to worry about because she hadn't lost me before.

I wasn't being fair to her at all. I didn't really care that she saw me that way. She was my mother and I had needed her. I was a little girl. I shouldn't have had to figure it all out on my own the way I had. She'd focused on Molly all the time. I wanted just a little bit of her time and attention.

Daddy did his best to make up for it but it just wasn't the same. I spent a lot of time alone or with my friends. Until Molly moved out. Then I started spending almost all of my time away from home with her at her apartment.

Molly and I had the best times at that apartment back then. We ate junk food and played a lot of board games. She didn't have much back then, so we sat on bean bag chairs and ate generic junk food. It didn't matter then. We just had so much fun in her little empty apartment with no furniture.

Molly didn't even have a bed, but she made me swear I wouldn't tell our parents. I never did, but I worried about her every single night. A few months after she moved in she'd found a free bed from some guy she knew. I wasn't so sure that was the best idea but she was super thrilled to have a bed. I didn't want to bring her down so I kept my mouth shut.

Momma asked about her every single day. How she knew that I went there as often as I did was beyond me. I never told her a thing other than Molly was fine. It wasn't really a lie because Molly was okay, she just wasn't doing as well as she needed to be.

I saw her fracturing more and more daily. Without Momma there to force her to go to therapy, she wasn't going at all. She told me that she'd had enough of all that head shrinking and wasn't interested in seeing Dr. Morales now. I tried to talk her into going, but she was adamant that she didn't need therapy.

I couldn't push too much or she'd push me right out the door. As long as I was allowed there with her, I could keep an eye on her. I hated that it felt like I needed to watch her but I did.

I was still thinking about Molly when my Mom called. I answered, prepared to argue only to find her crying on the other end.

"Momma, what's wrong?"

"Nothing. It's stupid. I just wanted to hear your voice and check on the girls. They were a little fussy earlier when Jason was here."

"They're fine. Jason put them down for bed already and they went down relatively fuss free."

"That's good. Maybe they were just tired from all the traveling back and forth today."

"Maybe. Want to tell me what's wrong now?"

"Nothing really. I was just thinking about when you and Molly were little and you fell and broke your arm. You cried so loud and Molly tried to put your arm back right, as she said. You screamed so loudly then. I had no idea what was going on when I ran out the door to find you screaming like Molly was killing you. She stood there holding your broken arm and you were crying so hard."

"I remember that. You yelled at her to let my arm go and it went limp because it was broken and I couldn't hold it up on its own."

"Yes, you're right. You were in so much pain and Molly was begging me to believe her when she said that she hadn't hurt you. I was so mad at her that your father came and took her inside while I raced you to the emergency room. It wasn't until later that night when I was putting you down for bed that you confirmed what she'd said. You told me not to be mad at Molly. Then you told me that you'd tried to climb the big oak tree and Molly tried to stop you but you fell and broke it that way. You were so scared that you'd get in trouble that you let Molly take the blame at first."

"But when I saw how mad you were at her, I had to tell you. I didn't want you to hate her because she was always so sad."

"You always thought about her feelings and did the right thing. Molly needed you more than she needed me. You gave her what I couldn't. You gave her unconditional love. I was so proud of you for that. I'm still proud of you for your compassion."

"Thank you, Momma. For calling. For saying that. For being you."

"Regardless of what you think, Lily, I do love you. I've always wanted you and loved you. You just didn't need me the way she did. You were so independent. You always knew exactly what you wanted."

"I still do, Momma."

"Yes, you do. You've always known. I never had to worry about you. I knew that you'd be okay."

"I guess I was pretty stubborn and headstrong, huh?"

"You still are."

We both laughed then. And fell into an easy banter, gossiping about everything going on in town. She told me all about Althea's son trying to sell the house. Ms. Althea had passed away a year prior and her only child, a son, had put the house on the market the day after she dropped dead. Momma told me all about the people that had been by to look at the house. He'd not had one offer since it went on the market.
She believed that it was priced too high and that the fact that Althea passed away in the house and wasn't found for over a week. Momma said her son hadn't bothered to have the house cleaned so the smell was still lingering. She said the entire neighborhood was aghast at the idea of poor Althea lying there and decaying.

I quickly told her that I didn't want to hear another word about it. We both agreed to table the Althea talk and she continued on about the new HOA leaders. Apparently they were demanding that everyone adhere to new rules about parking and guests. They didn't want people parking on the streets, saying it was killing the grass on the walkways.

Daddy had gotten into a very heated argument with the new president of the HOA. They threatened to fine Daddy for not cutting the grass to their exact specifications. He tore up the rules and regulations and threw them in the new president's face.

She went on and on about all of the changes they had implemented. No one was happy about any of it. The entire neighborhood had called for a new vote to overthrow the current HOA board.

I listened and said the appropriate things at the appropriate times. By the time we'd hung up I knew every single thing happening in her neighborhood. Funny how the little things were so important to you when the big things were gone.

I put my cell in my pocket after putting it on silent. I turned the tv on, found Gilmore Girls on Netflix and settled into the couch to let myself get lost in Stars Hollow with Loreliei and Rory. They always seemed to calm me and put me in a happy place.

I woke hours later to find a blanket over me and the tv off. I stretched and listened to the quiet of the house. I smiled to myself knowing that Jason had taken the baby monitor to bed with him so that I could have an uninterrupted night of sleep.

I settled back into the comfort of the couch and closed my eyes. I was sound asleep before I knew it.

I slept better than I had in a very long time. Momma and I had made up, the girls were quiet the whole night and Jason, well, he was an amazing man and husband. I woke to freshly brewed coffee, donuts and two little girls that had been fed, bathed and dressed for the day.

Molly and Daisy were happy and laughing when I entered the kitchen and I stopped to kiss them both on the top of the head before I took the cup of coffee Jason offered. I hesitated long enough to kiss him deeply then I took my first sip of coffee and took the donut he offered.

These kinds of mornings were the best kind. Everything was perfect and we had a quiet uneventful start to our day. I was beyond happy about it.

It wasn't always like this. Usually the girls were screaming and throwing food, Jason was rushing to drink coffee and inhale some type of breakfast and I was typically sitting in a chair quietly sipping my coffee and letting the morning take shape around me. I had no clue how I was going to do this for eighteen years.

I'd wanted children forever it seemed but now that they were here, I was realizing it was harder than I thought. I loved the girls, but two at once wasn't what I'd expected. Nothing in my life was turning out the way I'd anticipated.

I'd wanted to marry. I wanted to marry a man who gave me excitement and took me out of this town to someplace that no one knew who I was. I wanted to be somewhere where no one knew who Molly Anders was, or that I was her sister.

I wanted my own life. I wanted to be known as myself, not just the kid sister of the girl who was kidnapped. I wanted to be Lily and only Lily.

Now I was Mom and a wife. I'd never really had a chance to be Lily. I didn't even know who Lily was if I was honest with myself. I hated that I was never going to know who she was. I'd always be a mom now. I'd always be a wife to Jason.

I know it made no sense to think like that but that's how my brain worked when I was anxious or scared. I didn't have a clue why I was either of those things. I had no reason to be. I had a great life with a wonderful husband. So why wasn't I happy? Why did I feel trapped?

Chapter Seventeen

I had everything I thought I'd wanted. There was no way I'd walk away from it all. It wasn't in my nature to abandon my family. I may not always want to be here or be what I had become but I wasn't about to leave. This was my family and I was here to stay.

Jason looked at me questioningly. He knew me so well that he knew that something was going on. I shot him a smile and shook my head to let him know that it was nothing serious.

I put down my coffee and helped Daisy with her pancakes while Jason gave Molly another sippy cup of formula. These girls were growing too fast for my liking, but there was no stopping time.

We spent the day as a family. We took the girls out for a walk and then back home to play on their swing set that we'd given them for their birthday. They toddled around the yard, squealing with happiness while Jason and I chased them playfully.

We only stopped for lunch of dino nuggets and veggies for the girls and sandwiches for Jason and I. Then it was back outside to enjoy the last few days of summer. It would turn cold here soon and the girls would be cooped up in the house for far too long.

We skipped nap time that day. The girls would be cranky after dinner but they'd go down easily at bed time. They would certainly need a bath before bed but for now, we were having a grand time playing as a family.
Jason pushed them in the wagon. Both girls laughed and giggled all day long. It was the childhood they deserved. It was also the childhood my sister never got. It broke my heart to know that her childhood had been devoid of happiness like this.

I was so glad that my girls were getting to experience this life. I had wanted to give them everything the minute I found out that I was having them. These girls were my entire world and as much as I was tired and unsure of myself, my love for them was growing every single day.

By the time dinner rolled around we were all tired so Jason ordered a pizza while I cleaned the girls up for dinner. It was very rare that we ordered delivery because we both believed that the girls needed healthy foods more than anything. We always tried our best to feed them nutritious food, but pizza was one of our main food groups, so they may as well get used to it now.

Daisy and Molly were in their high chairs, bibs on, and happily drinking a bottle when the pizza arrived. Jason pulled a piece out of the box and tore it into small pieces for the babies. He put them on their plates and set them in front of the twins. They both reached for the pizza immediately.

Once I was satisfied that they were eating, I took the plate that Jason offered me. I inhaled the two slices and went back for more. The girls were babbling to themselves while Jason and I ate our dinner.

After we'd finished, we both headed up to give the girls a bath. It went much faster if one of us was ready with a towel and jammies while the other washed up the second child. Molly and Daisy both splashed in the water, laughing and playing as always in the bath.

They loved the water and I couldn't wait until we could take them to the ocean when they were older. We dressed them in their night clothes fairly quickly and got them settled into bed for the night.

We headed back downstairs to clean up from dinner, the baby monitor trained on the nursery. The girls were still sleeping in the same crib and held hands all night usually. They had settled down right away and were already asleep by the time we made it down the stairs.

"They were worn out for sure", Jason commented.

"Sure were," I said, gathering up the plates and washing down their high chairs. Jason had already started stacking dishes in the dishwasher. We were done in no time at all and he poured me a glass of wine, then opened himself a beer. We took our drinks to the living room and sat down on the couch, my head on his shoulder, and his hand on my thigh.

We were happy and in love. Nothing could break that. We sat there in silence, both tired from the day. I was both physically and emotionally exhausted. I wanted to turn in early but I didn't want to disconnect from my husband.

"You look like you're going to fall asleep any minute, babe. Should we go to bed?"

I nodded and let him lead the way, our glass and bottle left on the coffee table. I quickly washed my face and brushed my teeth, then threw on one of Jason's old tees to sleep in before crawling into bed. I was fast asleep before he even made it to bed.

I woke the next morning wrapped in his arms. The girls had slept through the night or Jason had gotten up with them because I never heard them. It was the best night's sleep I'd had in a long time. I was grateful for that because as the girls grew I was more and more tired.

I readied for my day and hurried to get the girls up. They were sitting up in their crib babbling to one another when I entered.

"Good Morning Molly. Good Morning, Daisy. Did you sleep well?"

I moved about the room, getting their clothes ready and laying out the diapers and wipes I'd need to get them prepared for their day. I picked Daisy up first and changed her, then dressed her before sitting her back in the crib. Then I moved on to Molly, going through the same routine with her.

Once they were both dressed, we went down to breakfast. I got them set up in their high chairs and gave them pancakes. These girls loved pancakes more than I did and I didn't think that was possible.

I watched them eat while the coffee brewed. The smell of coffee perked me up and I pulled the pot out from under the stream, sticking my cup under quickly. I never could wait for it to finish. Molly always teased me about that. I had a serious coffee addiction for a while and even now, I couldn't wait for it to brew before I got a cup.

The pot was back under the stream and I was stirring the Peppermint Mocha creamer into my cup when Jason joined us in the kitchen. The weekend was over and it was back to work for him. A tiny part of me envied him, that he got to leave and be among the adults outside of this house.

I loved staying home with the girls, but I was getting to the point that I wanted to go back to work soon. We'd talked about daycare but neither of us wanted our girls in daycare this early. We wanted them to socialize and learn but right now, we weren't ready to risk the germs and other kids. So until I could decide on someone to watch them, I was stuck here at home with the girls.

Not that I felt stuck all the time. Most days I loved being home with my girls. They were the best thing that ever happened to me and I loved them more than anything. It was just that some days I missed adult conversations. I was more than a little sick of Bluey and CocoMelon. These shows were not Blues Clues and thankfully the girls loved old episodes of Blue's Clues with Steve and Blue. It had been my favorite show as a child and now my girls loved it.

Even with Blue and Steve, I missed adult companionship. Going back to work had been the plan all along. I loved my job but I'd wanted to spend the first year with my girls. I wanted that bond to grow and be solidified. I was also terrified to let them out of my sight for long. When you're the sister of the girl who was kidnapped you were always worried.

That's what kept me home, knowing just how easy it is for someone to take your child in a matter of seconds. Every day on the news there were reports of missing children. My mind always raced to Molly and the life she'd been forced into. I prayed that every child would be found before those horrible things could happen to them, but in my heart I knew that they were probably already dead and if they weren't they were wishing that they were.

Over the last few years I'd read countless books and listened to countless audiobooks from women who had been abducted as children. Some of them had learned to live with their captors and felt that for the most part, they were treated well. Every single one of them talked about the sexual abuse that happened to them. Yet, every one of them forgave the people who took them.

It was the same story, over and over again. The man's wife or girlfriend helped him take the child. Or she knew about the girl and did nothing to help her. How were there women in the world who wouldn't help a child in that situation? Why would they want to stay with a man who would find sex with a child arousing?

I would never understand those women. I would never understand parents who didn't care for their babies and sold them to men or worse. The world was going to shit and quick.

I shook the thoughts from my racing mind because if I dwelled on them I'd never get anything done. I had to get the girls ready for their day and make a trip to the store at some point. We needed dinner ingredients and the girls needed new rain boots and I needed shampoo.

I just hated the idea of having to take them with me. It was so hard to shop with them because I was afraid to let them out of my sight for a second. It was irrational. I was aware. But go back a few paragraphs and read what I said about being the sister of the girl who was kidnapped.

Chapter Eighteen

Four hours later I was standing in the local WalMart having a panic attack because a Code Adam was called. I grabbed my girls and ran towards the doors. Somewhere in my mind I knew that they weren't going to let me out but there was no rational thought then for me. I held two screaming one year olds as tightly to me as I could without hurting them. The lady at the door must have recognized me because she motioned for someone to come take her place.

She calmly spoke to me telling me that everything was okay, that my girls were fine and we were just going to go sit down in the breakroom where we would be safe. We passed multiple people who stared at us and I should have been embarrassed but the only thought I had was that I had to keep my babies safe. I wouldn't be like my mother. I refused to let someone take my girls and use them the way she'd let Molly be used.

Had I been thinking rationally like a normal human being, I would never have thought those things, much less have said them to the kind lady who helped me. She spoke into the phone she carried, relaying that everything was okay and that she had me in the breakroom.

Somehow she'd managed to get me to tell her Jason's name and number and she called him to come to the store. I don't know how long we were back there in that break room or how long it took them to find the child that was missing but I could not let go of the girls. They were squirming and still screaming because they wanted to get down. I was sure that I was hurting them but I couldn't convince my arms to let go of them.

The lady, whose name I learned was LaVerne, spoke in such calming tones to me and the girls. She did her best to try to get me to let her hold one of the girls but I couldn't. I was overreacting. I knew this. She knew this. Everyone in the entire world knew this, but there was no way on this Earth I was going to let go of my girls while there was a child kidnapper in the area.

I would learn hours later that a child wasn't missing so much as his grandmother was "missing". Because they were unsure of where Grandma was in the store, they called a Code Adam and gave the child's description. I would find out later that he was twelve years old and autistic. The child was fine, he had no clue he was even missing. He was sitting with a lovely young woman in the middle of the book aisle, reading a story about Wild Things and where they were.

His grandmother would appear at the front of the store just minutes after I'd been taken to the back and she and her young grandson would be reunited. No harm. No foul.

Except....

That Code Adam being called had sent me into pure panic mode. As is the lingo today, I was triggered by that. I had a full blown panic attack and it didn't subside any until Jason was led into the room. Then, and only then, could I ease my grip on the girls a little. He tried to get me to give him Daisy and I fought him.

I stared right at him and told him that I didn't trust him. This man that had loved me through the worst times took those words and brushed them off like they were nothing. He showed love and patience that I didn't deserve then. An hour later I finally allowed him to take Molly from me. It made no sense at all to anyone, including myself, but I could not, nor would I, let go of Daisy. I kept mumbling about needing to protect her at all costs.

Dr. Morales would tell me later that I was suffering from PTSD but I didn't understand how or why, since I hadn't even been born when Daisy was taken. It didn't make sense how I could have a traumatic response to something that happened before my birth. She tried to explain that over the years, I'd absorbed the trauma from hearing about Molly's ordeal and living through her dissociative identity disorder. I had heard my mother go over and over the details of that day so many times, that in my own way I was living through it when she told it.

Another reason to be angry with my mother, I thought. She'd given me contact PTSD. I laughed to myself even though it wasn't funny in any way. I wasn't even the kid that got taken and here I was freaking out over someone else's kid being lost in a WalMart.

Jason drove us home the night I panicked. He helped me into the house, cautiously taking Molly, knowing that there was no way I was letting go of Daisy until we were safely behind the locked door of our own home.

Once inside I let go of the vice grip I had on her and hated myself for scaring both girls so much. I wish that I could say I fully understood what I had been thinking or doing, but in all honesty, I had no idea what had happened.

I let Jason change the girls and feed them. I sat so close to Daisy and Molly that they were both scared I was going to pick them up again. It would take weeks for them to not be afraid of me after that.

I hated myself so much for what I'd done. Jason, on the other hand, was so kind. He kept telling me that it wasn't my fault. He said that he understood but how could he when I didn't even understand myself?

He said that after everything that had happened in the last twenty-something years it was understandable that I'd have a panic attack when a Code Adam was called.

I sat with my head in my hands while the girls napped. I cried as hard then as I had the day Molly died. I worried that I was becoming mentally unstable like she was. I worried that I'd scarred my baby girls for life.

I wanted Jason to hate me for what I'd done. I wanted him to yell at me, scream, tell me I was stupid to think that someone would take the girls. I wanted that to be true. I wanted to never have lived with a sister who was taken. I wanted to go back in time and save Daisy the way I tried to save my girls today.

I wanted my mind to not immediately think that my children were in danger because someone called a Code Adam. I knew that Code Adam was in place to help quickly find a child that was missing. It was meant to save that child from the life that Molly had been dealt. I knew that it was a good thing to have in place and that John Walsh had fought hard to get that passed. He'd lost his son to someone who took him just like they'd taken Molly.
Only Molly was one of the "lucky" ones. She came home. John's little boy, Adam, came home in a body bag. Sometimes, I wondered if it would have been easier for Molly had she been killed right away instead of enduring six years of abuse. I wondered how my life would have been had Molly never returned. Would my parents still be looking for her or would they have given up after I was born?

Would I have been the replacement for the child that was lost?

I really didn't want to think about that but how could I not? If Molly hadn't come home, would they have loved me more? Would I have been the center of their world? Or would they have been so overprotective? Momma never worried too much about me because I was responsible even as a little girl but what if Molly had never been found? There is no way she would have treated me the same.

I often wondered if they were sad that she'd been found alive. With everything that she had put them through, wouldn't it have been better if they'd found her body instead of finding her alive? What those monsters had done to her was so horrible that they'd destroyed her mentally. It would have been kinder for them to have killed her.

God, what was I saying? I was wishing that she'd never come back. I was a horrible person and sister. I loved her, I really, truly did but being her sister had been Hell. This wasn't the first time, and I'm sure it won't be the last, that I wished she hadn't come home.

But if she hadn't, I wouldn't be who I was. I wouldn't have met Jason. I wouldn't have the girls. My whole life would be different and I wasn't sure I'd like that at all. I loved Jason. I'd loved him since the moment I met him. I loved our life together and how he brought me peace in an otherwise chaotic world. I loved that he never let me face anything alone, he was always at my side. He was my best friend, my lover, my husband, and so much more.

My girls were everything I'd ever wished for. They were beautiful and looked so much like their namesake that at times it was eerie. They may be identical in looks but their personalities were the polar opposite. Molly was outgoing and fun, laughing all the time and never afraid. Daisy was shy until she warmed up to you, and a little more reserved. I could see the fear she fought all the time. Molly pushed her to do things but Daisy always held back.

They were just like the Molly and Daisy who came before them. There were days that I loved how much they reminded me of my sister. Other days I hated it because it broke my heart to know that she wasn't here to meet them, to love them, to know them. They would never know her personally. They'd never see the kindness in her eyes or know that she would always have candy in her bag for them.

She would have been a great Auntie. Molly loved little kids. She wanted to protect them and keep them safe from people like Jim and Diane. She used to tell me that she dreamed about being a cop just so she could get people like them off the streets. She would have been great at it. Molly was great at anything she set her mind to. The only problem was that Daisy wasn't. Daisy had been so sheltered and was so shy and quiet. Everything frightened her. Men especially. She was never comfortable around a man. I think that subconsciously she knew what had happened to her and that was why she didn't like men.

Molly believed wholeheartedly that Daisy knew nothing and I think that she liked it that way. In her own way, she believed that if Daisy didn't know, then it hadn't happened to her.

I've spent so much of my life trying to figure it all out. I wanted to know why she'd been the way she had been. Why couldn't she just be a normal woman, without all the trauma. I spent years of my life questioning who she would have been had she not been taken. I would have had my big sister now I believed.

Perhaps she'd be married and have kids of her own and we'd have barbecues and sleepovers with the cousins. She would be happy and full of life. There wouldn't have been anything to worry about when we took the kids to the park because we'd never known that the world wasn't safe for kids. We'd just go about our lives, having coffee, chatting over brunch, watching the kids play. Never knowing that somewhere out there were people who got off on hurting little kids.

I think I would have preferred that world, if I were being honest. I think that Daisy would have too. Molly would never have needed to exist. Would I have liked the version of Daisy that could have been? Or would we be those kinds of sisters that saw each other on holidays only? I had no idea because those decisions were taken from us. We weren't given a chance to grow up totally normal.

Anytime I talked about wanting to be "normal" Daddy used to say that normal was just a setting on a washing machine, why would anyone want to be that?

It hadn't made much sense to me back then but now, as an adult, it sure did. I'd craved normality only to find out when I was grown that normal was an illusion. Everyone had their own issues and their own little weird things about them. All families were different. Some got along. Some hated each other. Some were broken. Some pretended to be just perfect.

In reality, no one was normal. Normal didn't exist.

⩾Chapter Nineteen⩽

Momma had heard all about what happened at WalMart and had come over first thing the very next day. I knew she'd called a few times because I'd heard Jason telling her that there was no need for her to come over. He had saved us all a lot of heartache that night.

She was here now though and treating me like a child once again. Today, I welcomed it. I needed to feel safe and comforted by my mother. I let her make breakfast and take care of the girls. I stayed in my pajamas and laid on the couch with a blanket. I didn't even turn on the tv for background noise like usual. I didn't want to let the outside world in. I wanted to exist inside these four walls, where we were safe and no one would ever try to snatch my kids. I wanted to know that no one could get in and the girls couldn't get out. We were safe here and only here.
The thoughts didn't sound rational even to me but right now it was what I needed to believe, so I believed it. I didn't move the entire day. Momma tried to get me to eat, I told her I wasn't hungry. She tried to make me tea, but I refused it. I drank water because I had to. I nibbled on peanut butter and crackers because she forced me to.

For the most part I just laid there and stared out the window at the world passing me by. Every time a car drove by and seemed to be going slow, I was convinced that they were going to pull into my drive and attempt to take my kids. I made Momma swear that she wouldn't open the door for anyone but Jason.

No, I wasn't thinking clearly or rationally. That was a given. Momma let me believe what I needed to to get through the day. She understood this feeling more than anyone could. She knew the fear that I'd felt because she'd felt it. Only in her case, her child was actually taken.

I'd never thought about how this had all affected her life and her mental health. I had only been concerned about myself and Molly but Momma had carried the guilt and fear for so many years now.

How had it been for her? Had she been scared that Daddy would blame her? Did she think that it was her fault? Did the police treat her like a suspect? Had she forgiven herself?

I knew that Daddy said he'd forgiven her because he believed it wasn't her fault but had he really? Had he treated her differently after Daisy was taken? Had she treated him differently? Did he believe she was capable of planning something like this with her own child?

Knowing my mother, there was no way she'd ever do something like that. It had all been a freak accident of her turning her back for a moment. But it was a moment that had cost my sister everything. Perhaps it cost my mother the same.

I wanted to ask her. I wanted to know. I needed to know but I was scared to death of the answer she might give. I didn't know what she had been like before Daisy was taken. I only knew the mother whose daughter came home after six years.

Daddy used to tell us that Momma was the most beautiful girl in the world. He called her Smiley because she smiled all the time. I barely remember her smiling at all as a small child. Surely he must be mistaken. Surely it hadn't changed her that much.

Oddly, my mother looked far older than her sixty-four years. Her face was etched with wrinkles that made her look sad all the time. If I had to guess, I'd say that Molly had been the reason for that sadness.

How did you ask someone questions about their feelings around a subject like this? Could I just outright ask her? Would she even tell me the truth? I know that I wouldn't tell anyone anything if they'd asked me. I'd want to protect myself and my child. I was sure that my mother would be the same.

She'd always been open and honest with us girls to a certain extent about Molly's disappearance. She told us the truth when it mattered and to mind our business when it hadn't. We weren't totally sheltered from what had happened but we were sheltered enough to know that we were safe and no one would hurt either of us now. Momma and Daddy both made sure of that. And for that I was grateful to them both.

"You've been awfully quiet in here," Momma said, scaring me enough that I jumped when she spoke.

"Sorry, I'm just thinking."

I hadn't let the girls out of my sight, even with her trying to take them to the other room to play. She'd been kind enough to listen when I asked her to let them stay in here with me. She's sat on the sidelines all day, only leaving to fix me a cup of tea or to clean some room.

"Talk to me, Lily. What's going on?"

"Did you ever forgive yourself?" I just blurted it out.

"For what happened to Daisy?" She paused to think about it in silence for a few minutes. "Yes, eventually I did. I still have times when I question everything I did that day. I question if I should have stopped at the store, or if I should have let her out of the cart."

"And what have you decided on?"

"There wasn't anything I could have done differently that would have changed anything. What happened was already written and I had to learn to live with that."

"So you think that what happened to Molly was just meant to happen? Isn't that kind of the easy way out?" I sounded angry because I was angry at her. I wanted to hate her so much. I wanted her to understand where I was coming from with this. I wanted her to see that her actions never helped any of us. It was her fault. It was all her fault and I hated her for what happened to my sister and how my life was fucked up because of it. I wanted her to understand that what she thought was meant to be had ended up destroying my sister and left me terrified that the same thing would happen to my girls.

"Lily, you're twisting my words. I never said that it was meant to happen. How could you think that of me?"

Her voice broke when she spoke. I wanted to believe what she was saying but I'd seen so much. I'd heard too many things over the years that hadn't made sense. I had way too many questions.

"Think about what you said, Momma. You said that you believed it was written already and you couldn't change it. That's bullshit. No way in Hell anyone wrote what happened to Molly."

"Lily, this has to stop. I've beaten myself up every day since she was taken. I wake up every day wondering what I could have done differently. I've begged God to turn back time. I've begged God to turn it back and let them take me instead. Do you seriously think I would ever do anything like that to Daisy? She was my daughter. I never gave up looking for her. Even when they told me it was hopeless. I would still be looking for her right now if she hadn't come home. I would never have stopped. Ever. Daisy was my world. Just like the girls are your's. Do you really think I'd stop looking for her? Or that I'd give her to someone who did the shit they did to her? If you do then you're not the woman I believed you to be."

"I'm exactly who you raised me to be. You raised me to ask questions and to never trust anyone. You did this Momma. You turned your back and your daughter was taken. You are the reason everything happened to her."

I was so mad and so fucked up then. This wasn't what I meant. It wasn't who I was. I didn't want to hurt her. I didn't want to do this but I couldn't stop now.

"Fuck you, Lily."

Before I knew what was happening the door was slamming behind her. I watched her sit in her car and cry. I stood there, just watching. I knew that everything I'd done was wrong. I knew that she had every right to hate me for what I'd accused her of.

It took her over an hour to gather herself and leave. She was on the phone before she left and as soon as she pulled out of the drive my phone rang.

"Lily, you had no right to speak to your mother that way."

My father's voice was calm and stern and that scared the Hell out of me. Momma had always said that if he was yelling, we were safe. Now, he was calm and he spoke so clearly.

"If you ever speak to her like that again, you will not be welcome in our home. You're my daughter, Lily, but you have no clue what we went through when your sister was taken. And I will never tolerate you disrespecting your mother again. Are we clear?"

"Yes, sir," I said.

He hung up without another word and I went back to my place on the couch watching the girls play. I was still there when Jason walked in the door.

"What the fuck happened today, Lily?" His voice was louder than normal and I turned to face him, eyes red and puffy from crying.

"I told Momma how I felt about the shit that went down with Molly."

"Damn it, Lily. What the fuck are you thinking? I understand that you lost it yesterday but you can't do this shit. You're going to ruin everything we've been working for."

"That's what you're worried about? You're kidding me, right? What have we been working for, Jason? A life that I don't even want? I'm not working for that. You just don't get it, do you? My fucking sister is dead. She killed her fucking self and that fucked me up. You want me to be this perfect little wife and mother. Guess what Jason, I'm not perfect. I can't be a replacement for your parents. I can't be the person you want me to be just because you want it. I am who the fuck I am."

'And who the fuck are you, Lily? Last I checked you were my wife and the mother of my children. Trust me, you couldn't hold a fucking candle to my mother, so don't even try. You're god damn lucky I took a chance on you after everything I'd heard about you."

'Fuck you. Fuck you, Jason. Everything you heard about me? It's all fucking true. Every fucking word of it is true. I'm a fucking mental bitch who spent way too much fucking time with her fucked up sister. Maybe you should have thought about that before you married me and had kids with me."

"Get the fuck out Lily. Get out until you can figure your shit out. The girls don't need you here like this. Go figure your shit out."

"You're kicking me out? This is MY fucking house, Jason. Did you forget that? There is no way in Hell I'm leaving this house or my kids. I'm not my mother. And you can kiss my ass if you think I'll ever let you take my girls away from me. I'll see you dead in Hell before I allow anyone to take them and do to them what happened to Molly."

"Do you even hear yourself? Listen to what you're saying, Lily. Do you seriously think that I'd ever hurt the girls? What the fuck is going on inside that head of yours? You have a brain, Lily, fucking use it. Stop this shit and get yourself together."

"Or what, Jason? What are you gonna do? Leave? Go ahead. There's the fucking door, but make sure you leave your fucking key because once you walk out of it, you ain't coming back."

I turned my back on him. I heard his key hit the table in the hall and the door slam behind him. I still didn't move when I heard his car peel out of the drive and I finally got up and picked up my girls. We went to the kitchen for dinner and the girls ate while I sat at the table, watching them.

I don't know what had gotten into me. Maybe I was having a breakdown. Maybe the stress of having to take care of Molly for all of those years and her suicide had taken it's toll on me. Maybe I was just crazy. Who the fuck knew anymore. All I knew was that there was no way I was going to let Jason take my girls away from me.

They were MY girls and I'd protect them at all costs. I couldn't protect Molly but I could protect her namesakes. I'd do anything to keep them safe.

Chapter Twenty

Weeks passed without a word from Jason. Until one day I was served with custody papers. He was suing me for full custody of the girls. He'd also filed legal separation papers. My marriage was over and he was trying to take my girls.

I couldn't call my family. They still weren't talking to me. So I called the only person who would understand why I'd finally lost it on everyone.

London picked up on the third ring. "Hey, Lily Bug, what's up?"

"I need help, London."

The pain and fear in my voice must have put him on edge. "Where and when?"

I gave him the address again and waited for the doorbell to ring. An hour later, I opened the door and he pulled me into that huge bear hug he always gave me when I showed up at Molly's apartment.

We'd been friends from the very beginning of their relationship. He'd been kind to me and he loved her and that was all that mattered in my mind.

We sat down with a cup of coffee while the girls napped and I spilled it all to him. I told him about how I broke down and questioned my mother and how I destroyed my marriage all in the same night. He listened without interrupting and when I was done he sat his coffee mug down and asked the most important question.

"So, what is it you want, Lily? What did all of that accomplish for you? Do you feel better now?"

"No. I don't know what I expected but it sure wasn't this."

"Why did you do it?"

"Because I'd had a bad day. I needed to vent and she was there."

"So you just decided to drop that bomb on your momma, the woman who has been through it more than anyone since Molly was little and then you thought you could walk away unscathed?"

"I don't know."

"Sounds to me like you didn't expect it to all blow up in your face."

"I guess that I didn't. I sure didn't expect to end my marriage over this shit."

"Lily, you have to find a way to forgive her."

"My mother?"

"No. You have to find a way to forgive Molly. And let her go. You're fighting a ghost now. She's gone and nothing that we do is going to bring her back."

"I'm not mad at Molly. She did nothing wrong," I argued.
"Are you sure you believe that, Lily?" He waited a few beats before he continued. "I was angry at her too. I wanted to hate her for not having the courage to fight. She did something that was so selfish and I was angry as fuck about it. We were supposed to get married, have a family and a life together. I was ready to help her deal with all of the trauma from her past. I loved her. Hell, I still love her. I'm still IN love with her. I'll always be in love with her. I'm just not angry with her anymore."

I was sobbing by the time he'd finished speaking. I knew that he would understand what I'd been feeling. He'd been there through some of the worst times with Molly. He'd fought for her as much as I had. He'd loved her as deeply as I had.

"Listen, Lily, it is okay to be angry with her. You're entitled to feel that what she did was wrong. Even with everything that we know, we are still human. We still are allowed to be pissed off and hate her for leaving us here to deal with the aftermath. We will never fully grasp or understand what was happening in her mind or soul. We don't know the full extent of the abuse and trauma she lived through. We know what was told to us and we think about how we would react, but we have no idea what her life was like when it was happening. As much as she told us, there was so much more that she didn't. And that is okay. She didn't have to tell us anything. She certainly was entitled to not be able to feel emotions like love but somehow she did. She found her way through that darkness to love us and I for one am eternally grateful. She loved you so much, Lily. She was proud of you and all you'd do in the world. She wouldn't want you to be going through all of this. If she were here, she'd be sitting here holding your hand and loving you through it. We both know that."

"I know," I said through my tears, sniffling. "She had so much love to give."

"That she did and we were lucky enough to be on the receiving end of it. She still amazes me that she survived everything that she did. I can't even imagine the fear and hatred she had inside of her but somehow she managed to overcome that and allow love into her life. A large part of that is due to the love and concern your mother showed her when she came home. She often talked about how she wouldn't have been able to make the progress that she had without Amy. I think that she felt guilty that she put her through the pain and loss that she had but she understood through therapy that it wasn't her fault. Molly never blamed your mother and neither should you. She worked very hard to move past that idea. She wanted very much to learn to forgive and love. That was part of her reasoning for wanting to see Jim one last time. She wanted the closure, to end it on her terms and no one else's. That's who she was, Lily. She knew that the person she was was because of all that Jim had put her through. She wouldn't be Molly without it. I don't know how Daisy would have done because she wasn't in charge very often. I do know that Molly loved her and wanted to protect her at all costs. I also know that Emma-Lee loved Daisy completely. Every day of her adult life, she was loved. In the end that was all that mattered."

"I'm so mad at her. She left me here with no idea how to survive without her. How do I get past that?"

"It takes time and work on your part. You have to be committed to therapy and asking for help. One of the things I did was write letters to her with all that I was feeling and then I burned them and released the ashes. It was a visual representation of letting those feelings go. You have to find what works for you. You'll know when you find it."

"I don't know." I was worried that I'd never be able to forgive her. I hadn't even realized how much of my time and energy being angry at her was consuming. I'd ruined my marriage and my relationship with my family by being angry at my sister for dying.

"Look, it's not going to be easy. You're going to have to make apologies and some people aren't going to forgive you. That's okay too. It's not on you to force them to do so. Your job is to ask for the forgiveness and explain why you did what you did and how you are working to correct those problems that led you to that place anyway. If they don't forgive you, that's on them. No one can make someone accept an apology. It's a very tough lesson to learn but it's an important one to learn for sure. Give yourself grace and patience. You deserve that at the very least."

"Thank you," I said, hugging him. We'd been friends for a long time now and I hadn't realized how much he had come to mean to me.

"No thanks necessary. You're family. You're like my kid sister, and I'd like to think that Molly would want me watching after you. She'd also want me to tell you to do whatever it takes to fix your marriage because it's obvious to everyone that Jason loves you very, very much. You have children now. You can't just throw away a life you've built because you lost your way. Beg him if you have to. If he's the man I think he is, he's probably waiting for you to reach out right now. Don't make him wait too long or you may lose him forever. Men like Jason won't be single long."

"I know. I love him just as much and I want this to work. I want our life back. I miss him. I didn't even realize how much until right now. I'll call him shortly, right after I call Dr. Morales and make an appointment as soon as humanly possible."

"I think if you tell her what's been happening, she will get you in right away. She helped Molly through so much that I'm sure she's just been waiting for you to reach out when you were ready. Now is the time, Lily. Reach out. Talk to her, be truthful and you'll find that things get a lot easier inside that head of yours. I'm here if you need me. Always."

"Thank you, I appreciate that and thank you for coming over when I needed to talk. No one else understands where I'm coming from on this."

"I always got you, Lily. I gotta run, Molly has a play at school and I promised her I'd be there on time for a change. You should call your mom and try to repair that relationship before you even begin to work on Jason. Call Dr. Morales first thing in the morning."

He kissed my cheek and hugged me goodbye before he left. I sat there on the couch thinking about everything he'd said until the girls woke from their naps. I finished out our day, playing with them, going on our late afternoon walk and then made dinner for us. Once bathtime was done and the girls were down for the night, I picked up the phone and dialed my mother's number.

She answered on the fourth ring, right before the voicemail picked up. I was sure she'd sat there debating on whether she wanted to answer or not. I was glad that she did.

"Momma, before you hang up, I wanted to say I'm sorry. I am deeply sorry for the things that I said and accused you of. I'm not in a good place right now but that's not an excuse for what I said or did. I wanted to hurt you. I know it was wrong but I wanted you to feel as bad as I did. I would like for you to forgive me but if you don't, I understand. I don't need an answer tonight or even any time soon. Regardless of how you feel about me, the girls deserve to know you and you deserve to know them. Please don't penalize them for what I've done. I can arrange for someone to bring them to you or however you want to deal with it but please don't shut them out. They love you and they need you in their lives."

I waited for her to respond but she didn't so I spoke again.

"Okay, Momma, I'm gonna go now. Think about what I said. You can have someone else reach out to me if you need to. I love you. Good night."

I hung up and held back the tears that threatened to fall. She'd listened to me and that was a start. I'd be honest with her about the girls, I wanted them to know her. I'd been so disrespectful to her and I regretted it. I couldn't take it back because once the words are spoken, they are forever. The best I could hope for was that she'd heard me and would accept my apology. I wanted my mother back but I truly understood that that may never happen.

I went to bed that night knowing that tomorrow would be harder. I had to talk to Jason and convince him that I was truly sorry. It would devastate me if he didn't forgive me. We'd been together for so long that I didn't remember who I was without him. We'd been building a life together. We'd started a family, out of love, and now we weren't even living in the same home. How had things gotten this bad?

I could only hope that London was right, that apologizing and admitting I need help was a step in the right direction. If not, then I had no idea how I was going to get through this. I needed my husband. I needed him to support me and love me through this all.

I wasn't sure that I was strong enough to do this without him but I was willing to try if I had to. I barely slept that night, tossing and turning all night. By 4am, I decided to just get up and start the day.

I headed downstairs and made a pot of coffee. I sat at the kitchen table and drank it in the dark, listening closely for the girls to wake up. It was going to be a few more hours at the very least so I sat there, in the silence of the kitchen, drinking my coffee.

My mind raced with thoughts of how I was going to approach this all with Jason. I tried to think about what I wanted to say to him. I thought about how I needed to convince him that I was being honest and really wanted to work on our marriage. I wanted our life back.

At the very least, I wanted to make sure that he saw the girls. They missed him so much and so did I. We'd been through so much together. There was no way that we should end this over something so stupid.

He'd been right to react the way he did. I deserved it but I knew that he loved me and I loved him. We had to be able to work this out. It would be hard but we could do it if we tried.

I wanted him to come home. I wanted him to see the girls every day. I wanted him to still love me. As I sat there, I came to realize that all I kept saying was what I wanted. I hadn't stopped to think about what Jason or my mom would want. What if they didn't want to repair the relationship with me?

How would I handle that? What if Jason had moved on? London was right. Jason wasn't the kind of man that would stay single for long. He was kind and thoughtful. He was handsome and successful. He was the perfect man and I'd basically driven him away.

And I had no idea why.

Chapter Twenty-One

By the time the girls woke I was on my last cup of the pot of coffee. I'd cleaned the kitchen and living room, tidied up my bedroom and thrown in a load of laundry. I was just transferring the load from washer to dryer when the girls woke up.

I hurried to get them up and changed for the day then we went down for breakfast. The girls babbled to one another as they shared food across their high chairs. It amazed me at how they were always in sync with one another. Being identical twins had a lot to do with that I was sure, but regardless, I loved to watch them interact. Their little personalities kept me on my toes for sure.

It had been a lot easier with Jason here to help. I stopped dead in my tracks at the thought. In that moment, standing in the kitchen, I realized just how deeply I missed him. I had to fix things between us. I could only hope that he wanted to fix them. I wasn't sure how I'd survive him not wanting to stay married to me. We'd been through so much together in such a short time.

I pushed the thoughts away, turning my attention back to my girls. I couldn't dwell on what ifs. I had to face things head on now. The morning was flying by with the girls needing different things, cleaning up this disaster I'd let the house become, and listening to the news in the background half-heartedly. It was a busy morning and when I glanced at the clock I realized it was past time for Dr. Morales to be in her office. I searched for my cell phone and dialed her office number, asking the polite receptionist for the first available appointment. When she told me that it was four months out I begged her to speak to Dr. Morales as soon as she could to see if she could squeeze me in earlier and took the appointment that was available four months later.

Hours passed by and I was totally wrapped up in some show on the television when my phone buzzed. I looked at the text message, happy to see that Dr. Morales could fit me in the following week. I texted back my confirmation of the appointment and went back to the show.

I woke an hour later to the girls babbling away in their cribs. I hadn't realized just how tired I had been the last few days. I'd needed that nap it seemed but it was time to get up and take care of my life and my girls.

Daisy and Molly were so active that afternoon that I never got a chance to call Jason. Dinner time was chaotic with the girls throwing their food at one another and screaming the entire time. The rest of the evening went the same way. I told myself that they were just acting out because of all the changes that had happened in such a short time. They were missing their Nana and their Daddy. I understood that. I also understood that they didn't know how to communicate that other than the screaming and chaos that was happening.

Putting them down for the night took a very long time just due to how upset that they were over everything. I wanted to help them. I wanted to make them see that this wasn't going to be forever. This wasn't the life they were going to have to get used to.

I finally got them settled down an hour and a half after their normal bed time and closed the door quietly behind me. I turned on the monitor the moment I got downstairs so I could watch them. They both sat up in the cribs and moved so that they could put their arms through the slats and hold hands. Once they were hand in hand, they settled in and went to sleep.

They were built in best friends and it made me smile to think that they'd have each other for the rest of their lives. They'd never be alone in the world because they'd been born with their person. How wonderful that thought was.

I settled into the couch and took out my cell to call Jason. I hated how scared I was to call him. I was terrified that he hated me now and wouldn't even answer me, let alone take the time to talk to me about everything that had been going on. My hands trembled as I scrolled through the phone and found his contact, hitting dial before I could chicken out.

The phone rang several times before going to voicemail. His voice sounded warm and comforting as he asked me to leave a message.

"Hey Jason, it's me, Lily. Listen, I'd really like to talk to you and the girls really miss you. Can you please give me a call when you get this message? Doesn't matter how late it is. For what it's worth, I miss you too."

I mashed the button to hang up and put my phone down on the couch. It was going to be a long night as I waited to see if he was going to call me back. I worried that he wouldn't. Jason could be stubborn but I was persistent. I'd give him til lunch tomorrow then I was calling him back.

I took myself up to bed around ten and had another restless night. I wasn't sure I'd ever sleep soundly again. This situation I'd created had me completely at a loss and was taking its toll on me rather quickly.

Morning came way too early for my liking but I was able to get a couple of cups of coffee in before the girls woke for the day. We were just settling into breakfast when the doorbell rang and my heart jumped. I held my breath, hoping it was Jason. I straightened my hair and tried my best to look rested when I opened the door.

"Hey Lily girl." My dad's voice was calm and he sounded like the father I'd always known and loved. "Can I come in?"

I moved aside to let him in, closing the door behind trying not to let my disappointment show.

"Girls are having breakfast," I said, leading the way to the kitchen.

Daisy and Molly both squealed happily to see Papa, their little arms outstretched trying to convince him to pick them up.

"Girls, Papa will pick you up after you finish your breakfast."

Daddy studied their yogurt and fruit and smiled. They'd already thrown most of the cheerios on the floor but they were happily mushing the blueberries and mango between their little fingers. Molly had yogurt in her hair and blueberries on her nose while Daisy's little hands were purple from all the fun she was having smushing the berries.

"What's up Daddy?" I asked, wondering why he was here so early on a Thursday.

"Your mom told me that you called and apologized. That took a lot of courage and I'm glad you did it."

"But," I asked when he hesitated.

"She's not ready to forgive you just yet. Or maybe she's forgiven you but hasn't forgotten it yet. Either way, I didn't want you over here thinking that she wasn't going to respond to you at all. She did hear what you said about the girls, and she would love to see them when it's convenient for you. I can come pick them up or meet you somewhere. It's just not a good idea for you to come by the house just yet."

My heart sank. I had hoped she'd see that I was really trying and I meant what I'd said. It wasn't my place to tell her when to forgive me. I knew that but I was heartbroken that she still hated me.

"Okay." It was all I could muster up.

"Lily, this isn't going to last forever. Your momma loves you very much. She's just very hurt right now by what you said. She needs a little more time. I think that if she spends some time with the girls, she will see that she misses you."

"It's fine, Dad. I get it."

I turned my back to him and started loading the dishwasher with this morning's dishes while he played with the girls. I didn't want him to see the tears welling up in my eyes. I'd known that this was a possibility so I shouldn't have been caught so off guard by my mother's reaction.

We remained there in silence for a while. It wasn't comfortable but it wasn't hostile either. We were stuck somewhere in between where we had been as a family and where we were a few days ago.

"I have an appointment with Dr. Morales next week," I said. I was unsure why I wanted him to know that but hopefully it would help change my mother's mind about seeing me. "You're welcome to come get the girls that day, if you'd like. I'd just like them back home before dinner."

"I can do that. Can you pack them a bag so that we have everything that we need?"

"Sure. But Dad, I don't want them to leave your house except for going there and coming home."

"Lily, that's not fair."

"Life isn't fair, Dad. We all learned that when Molly died."

It was the last thing I said to him that day. She could keep me shut out but she couldn't make me accept certain things when she saw my girls. I could, and would, stop her visits if she didn't follow the rules.

My father stayed and played with the girls, giving me a chance to run up and shower while he was there. The girls had a great time with him and cried when he got up to leave. He gave them both kisses and hugs and promised he would see them the next week.

I saw him to the door and closed it behind him, locking it. I was angry and hurt. I knew that this entire thing was my fault for what I'd said to my mother, however, I didn't care. She was my mother. She shouldn't turn her back on me. It made me question everything that I'd said to her all over again.

Just once in my life, I wanted my mother to choose me, to choose to make me a priority and to accept me for my flaws and for who I was. She accepted Molly. She accepted Daisy. She accepted all the fucked up shit that Molly and Daisy had done but she couldn't accept that I had a breakdown and said some shit that she didn't like.

She shut me out. Refused to speak to me. Sent my father to tell me that she accepted seeing the girls but not me. So very typically my mother. It didn't matter that I'd apologized or that I'd lived through the worst of Molly's shit too. She still chose to shut me out.

Maybe London was wrong. Maybe I didn't need to make amends with her. She obviously didn't want to make amends with me. She didn't even want to speak to me. Her own daughter.

I was getting angrier by the minute. I needed to stop thinking about my mother and all of the times she chose anything and anyone other than me.

I put her out of my mind and focused on my girls and the things we needed to get done that day. There was no sense ruining their day with my issues. I swore a long time ago that I would be a better mother than the one I had. If I continued to dwell on all of this bullshit, I'd be just like her.

The morning went by quickly with the girls toddling around and getting into everything. After lunch, they went down easily for their nap. I stood there watching them sleep for a very long time. I was lucky to be their mommy. They'd given me a purpose, a reason to continue on. I loved them unconditionally.

I finally forced myself to leave their room and went to find my cell. I had sworn I'd call Jason after lunch if I hadn't heard from him. I was an hour behind on that and was doing my best to work up the courage when my phone rang. Glancing at the screen, my heart skipped a beat when I saw Jason's name there.

"Hello," I said, sounding a little out of breath.

"Hey, Lily, am I catching you at a bad time?"

His voice sounded like angels singing to me. "Nope, sorry, I just wasn't expecting it to be you."

"Oh, well, yeah. Listen, I think we should talk. Can you get a sitter and meet me sometime this week?"

"Um, sure. Did you have a day in mind?"

"Can you make it tomorrow for lunch? I have a meeting in the morning, but I should be free by one if you can make it."

I hesitated briefly, glancing at my calendar before I answered. "Yeah, I can make that work I think."

"Great. Let's meet at Antonio's then."

"Sounds good. I'll see you then."

"See you then. Bye."

And with that he hung up the phone. It concerned me a little that he was the one who wanted to talk. What if he was going to ask for a divorce? Would I be able to handle that? Would I break down and cause a scene? I think he was banking on that not happening in public and maybe that's why he wanted to do it at Antonio's. It was my favorite lunch spot and he knew I wouldn't do anything to ruin my chances of going there again.

I found myself worrying and wondering what he wanted to talk about the rest of the day. I did a quick clean of the house while the girls napped and called a friend to watch the girls the next day. She'd watch them here at the house since I'd only be gone an hour or so. Normally I wouldn't ask anyone to watch them other than my parents but with the tension between us, I didn't think it would be a good idea.

The rest of the day went by in a blur. The girls were getting more and more active and always needed something so I didn't have much time to sit down and rest lately. I'd started looking into putting them into a daycare program a few days a week so they could get some socialization and I could get some much needed time alone. I was even thinking about getting a part time job just to cover the cost of it since I wasn't working currently and I'd just about depleted my savings. I didn't want to touch the money that Jason put into our accounts so I simply withdrew the amount I had saved up from my job before having the girls and opened my own account.

A part of me had needed to be independent from him, from our marriage, this life we'd had together. I wasn't sure why I'd needed it but I had. Now that I had that independence I wanted to be back where I had been. I wanted to be Jason's wife again.

I had no clue if he wanted our marriage to work or if he was simply done. I wasn't even sure that I fully wanted what I wanted. Sometimes, you just can't figure it out because both options are filled with different blessings.

Chapter Twenty-Two

The next day I prepared far too long for lunch with Jason. I dressed in my favorite skirt, the new tank I'd bought about a month ago and a pair of flats. I put my hair up and touched up my makeup one last time before I ran down the stairs to give the baby last minute instructions for the girls. They'd be down for their nap by the time I got home so I explained how Daisy needed her ducky and Molly needed her doll to fall asleep. I gave strict instructions to not allow them to have any sweets or they wouldn't go down for their nap.

After a quick kiss for the girls, I grabbed my bag and keys and headed out. I drove slowly, partly because I didn't want to get there too early and partly because I was afraid that by the end of lunch my marriage would be over for good.

Once I got to Antonio's, I found a parking spot near the restaurant and tried to prepare myself for anything that could happen in the next hour. I found my courage and I got out of the car and walked towards the door of the restaurant that we'd had our first official date at.

Once inside, the hostess advised that Jason hadn't arrived yet but she could seat me right away. I settled into the small booth and ordered a glass of Malbac, hoping it would calm my nerves before Jason arrived. I went ahead and ordered Bruschetta as an appetizer as well.

The wine and appetizer had just arrived when Jason sauntered in like he wasn't ten minutes late. The hostess led him to our booth and he frowned when he saw the glass of wine in front of me. He stayed silent and slid into the seat across from me.

"Good to see you, Jason," I said and picked up my glass, taking a small sip just to prove a point.

"You too, Lily." He slid out of his jacket and folded it up, placing it on the bench next to him. "How are Daisy and Molly?"

"Growing fast, you should make a point to come by and see them soon."

"Yeah, I will set something up."

The waitress stopped by and he ordered a bourbon on the rocks and took a bite of the bruschetta.

"So, what's up, Jason?" I waited, holding my breath, terrified of what he was about to say.

"Lily," he paused, looking years older than he had a few weeks ago. "What is going on? Are we really doing this?"

"Doing what, Jason? I'm just trying to live my life and take care of our daughters. You're the one who left."

"Because you pushed me out the door. Have you gotten help?"

"Maybe I don't think I need help. Maybe, I'm good with how things are."

I had no clue where the hell this was all coming from. It certainly wasn't what I wanted to say to him. It wasn't anywhere near what I felt. I had to stop sabotaging my own life before I lost everything that mattered to me.

"God Damn It, Lily. Why do you always make things so much harder than they have to be? I came here willing to work on this marriage because I love you and I love our family. I hate living in hotels. I don't want to eat alone. I want to be in my house, with my wife and kids. I just need to know that you're trying to figure out what led to this breakdown you seem to be having."

"It's not a breakdown. I'm not Molly."

"Well you're sure acting like her right now."

"Fuck you, Jason. You didn't know her and you have no right to judge her. For your information, I'm seeing Dr. Morales starting next week. I have some things I need to work through but I'm doing what I need to do to be a good mother to my children. I even called and apologized to my mother, not that she cared in the least little bit. I was going to call you and apologize before you decided to bring me here and insult me. I don't want our marriage to end. I love you, in spite of myself at this point."

"I'm glad you're going to talk to someone. Your mother just needs some time to digest it all. She's been through a lot."

"So have I, Jason. I took care of Molly for years. When no one else was around, I was the one to listen to her, to hug her, to love her. It wasn't easy for me, either. Being Molly's sister was hard. Harder than anyone knew."

"I imagine it was. I never said it wasn't hard for you. You've been through a lot of traumatic stuff with her."

"She was my sister. I loved her."

"I know. But now it's time for you to love Lily. I want my wife back."

"I haven't gone anywhere, Jason. I've always been right here."

It was then that the waitress decided to come take our order. Jason ordered his usual fettuccine alfredo with chicken and I ordered the lasagne.

"I know that," he said as soon as she'd left to put our lunch order in. "I want to come home, Lily. I miss you. I miss the girls."

"We miss you, too, but I'm not sure if right now is the best time."

"I'll sleep in the basement. I just want to be home and help with the girls. I want to help you too, Lily."

By the end of lunch, we agreed that Jason would come home and stay in the guest room. It was a step in the right direction with enough time for us to really work on this marriage. We needed more than a lunch to figure it all out but we were willing to try and that's what mattered.

Jason showed up just before dinner. The girls were so excited to see him. They danced around and squealed with glee when he picked them up and gave them kisses all over. They were daddy's little girls for sure.

Daisy and Molly played more than they ate at dinner and I didn't argue when Jason offered to give them their bath before bed. He'd missed out on so much the last few weeks that I wanted the girls to have some time alone with him.

"They are down for the night," he said, smiling, when he came back downstairs. "They didn't even fight. One bedtime story, some kisses and cuddles and they were out like a light."

"That's great. There is wine in the fridge and I just put a new bottle of bourbon on the bar cart."

"Thanks," he said, going to the bar cart to pour himself a drink. He sat down across from me.

We sat in comfortable silence with our drinks. I scrolled through my phone, looking at daycares for the girls, trying to decide if I actually liked any of them. I wasn't focused on what Jason was doing at all so I didn't notice when he got up and went to bed.
At least I assumed he went to bed. I was used to being by myself now that I hadn't realized that perhaps he had wanted to talk. This was the only time I had to myself and I got wrapped up in what I needed to get done.

This wasn't the way I wanted our nights to be. I had wanted to be fully present so that we could work on this marriage. I would apologize in the morning and do my best to be more present from here on out.

I glanced at my watch, seeing it was almost eleven so I got up and turned off the lights, double checked the door locks and headed upstairs to bed. I slept horribly thinking about him in the guest room. My body betrayed me by wanting him. He was so close. I wanted to go to him. I wanted my husband but I stayed put in our bed, tossing and turning the entire night. I'd already messed up so many times that I didn't want to mess up anymore.

I wanted this to work and I was willing to do whatever it took to make it work. This was just the beginning and I wasn't going to screw it up this time. I stared at the ceiling for most of the night. Time passed by extremely slowly.

At some point I fell asleep out of sheer exhaustion and I woke to sunlight pouring into the bedroom. I stretched and looked over at the clock and nearly had a heart attack when I saw it was 10am. I looked for the baby monitor and couldn't find it. How had I slept through the girls waking up? And why weren't they up yet? Something had to be wrong.

I raced down the hall without my robe or stopping to pee. The girls weren't in their room and my anxiety got worse. Where were my girls? What had happened to them?

I tore down the stairs only to find the girls playing happily in the living room with Jason sitting on the couch reading the paper. Once I started breathing again, I ran a hand through my hair and went back upstairs to shower and dress before I had a major breakdown. I let it go in the shower, crying and getting it all out. It was what I needed. By the time I got out of the shower I felt so much better.

I dressed casually then headed back downstairs for a cup of coffee. Jason turned to look at me again when I arrived back downstairs.

"Everything okay?"

"Yeah," I said, walking toward the kitchen. "I just didn't realize that I'd slept so long."

"When you didn't get up for the girls, I figured you must be exhausted since you've been doing it all alone lately. Thought I'd let you sleep in for a change."

"Thanks, I appreciate that," I called out from the kitchen, where I was pouring my first cup of coffee for the day. I looked around, surprised to see it so clean. Even the high chairs were put away. I took my coffee back to the living room, stopping to kiss the girls.

"What did they have for breakfast?"

"Yogurt and fruit," Jason replied. "Molly doesn't really seem to like strawberries."

"No, she refuses to eat them. I think it's the seeds."

"Could be. Daisy loved them though."

"Isn't it weird how they are so identical and yet one hates strawberries and the other loves them?"

It was more of a statement than a question and we sat in comfortable silence for a while.

"Are you not working today?" I asked out of curiosity. I wasn't used to Jason being home at this time of the day and it worried me just a little.

"I took a couple of days off since I was moving back. I wanted to spend some time with the girls since I haven't seen them in so long."

"They will love that. Did you have plans for you three?"

"I thought I'd take them to the zoo tomorrow. I just wanted to relax and let them get used to me being here again today. Is that okay?"

"That's perfect, actually. I have to go to the grocery anyway so that will give me a chance to go alone and not have to rush."

"Great." He hesitated a few moments, then looked over at me. "You can come to the zoo with us if you want?"

"No, no, that's okay. You should take the girls and have fun with them. They need some daddy daughter time. It will be good for all of you."

"Are you sure?"

"Jason, you don't have to include me in your time with the girls. Even if we hadn't had any problems that happened, I'd expect you to spend time with the girls alone. It's good for all of you."

He nodded and dropped the subject.

I left him to bond with our children and went upstairs to work on some stuff I'd been wanting to get done. I managed to strip the sheets from my bed and the girls cribs and wash them all. I remade the beds with clean bedding, vacuumed the entire upstairs, cleaned the upstairs bathrooms and the girls' room. I went through their closets and pulled out all the clothes that no longer fit and packed them away to take to the consignment shop later in the week.

I forgot about lunch and was just about to dive into my closet when Jason brought up a sandwich for me. I looked at my watch and was shocked to see how late it was.

"Thank you," I said, taking the sandwich and taking a bite hungrily. "I didn't realize it was so late. I planned on coming down to fix lunch for the girls. Did they eat and go down for their nap?"

"Yes, I made them some chicken with fruit and green beans. Got them cleaned up, changed and down for a nap about ten minutes ago."

"Thank you, again."

"You're welcome. You seemed busy, so I just handled it."

WIthout another word he left the room, closing the door behind him. I ate the sandwich and chugged the bottle of water he'd brought along with it. I was happy to let him take care of the girls until dinner time.

I went back to tackling my closet, tossing out clothes I didn't wear anymore. They'd all go to the donation pile at the domestic violence shelter after I dropped off the girls clothes at the consignment shop. I would go shopping for them later on when I had a little more time. The alarm I'd set went off and I finished up quickly so I could go down and make dinner.

I was standing at the stove making spaghetti and meatballs for dinner when Jason popped in to check on how long until dinner. I told him ten minutes and went back to cooking while he brought the girls in and started putting them in their seats.

I mixed their spaghetti with the sauce and cut the meatballs up for them into bite sized pieces. I spooned it straight onto the tray of their high chairs. They picked it up, looking at it before tasting it. By the squeals of happiness they emitted, they apparently liked it.

Then again, who didn't like spaghetti and meatballs? I made Jason a plate, adding a salad and garlic bread before handing it to him. He thanked me as I brought my own plate to the table, sitting in my usual spot.

We ate quietly, both watching the girls and laughing at how they were covered in spaghetti by the time they were done. Jason and I both grabbed a twin and took them upstairs to bathe them one at a time. Jason did the bathing while I dried and dressed the clean one for bed.

Both girls were ready to play and not sleep. I put them in the same crib for the first time in a while, letting them play and babble to one another in the language they seemed to share. Most days I had no idea what they were saying but they seemed to be talking things out.

Jason and I stood in the doorway, taking it all in.

"They are growing so fast," I said when we were on the couch later. "I can't believe they are already a year old."

"They've grown so much since I saw them last. They are doing really well though. That's mostly because of you."

"Thank you," I said sincerely. "I've done my best to be a good mom for them. They deserve that at the very least."

"Well, you are better than a good mom, Lily. Our girls are thriving and so smart. It's nice to see that they are as happy as they are."

"I've been looking into daycares. I want them to get some socialization so that when Pre-K comes around, they are ready to learn."

"I think that's a great idea. Have you found any that you like?"

"I have, actually. There is a place over on Main that has amazing reviews. I thought I'd stop in on Monday after my appointment with Dr. Morales. I want to talk to their director and maybe look into the classrooms. I also want to see their licensing and inspections before I agree to anything."

"Sounds like you're ready to give them the once over and make sure they are the best place for our twins."

"That's the plan. If you want to, you can meet me there. I'm sure you have questions for them too."

"Thank you, I think I'll take you up on that invitation."

The rest of the night was spent in comfortable conversation that didn't go too deep. We were on the right track with him being here. I was enjoying his company even if we weren't completely back together. At the very least we were trying to coexist in the same home. Daisy and Molly seemed much happier as well. That was a bonus for sure.

⩾Chapter Twenty-Three⩽

Jason was up early, preparing for his day with the girls at the zoo. I was up right alongside him, packing them snacks and bottles so that they didn't lose their shit on him and throw a tantrum inside the gorilla exhibit. I included snacks for Jason as well. It was going to be a very long day for him with two one year old girls at the zoo. I reminded him to take the double stroller and to make sure the girls wore sunscreen and it was reapplied often.

I packed their hats and glasses, a change of clothes for each of them, extra diapers and shoes and socks. Jason hadn't really spent a full day out with the girls since they'd been born. He was in for a crash course in twins and I was afraid it wasn't going to be pretty.

I packed a few extra bottles of water, extra cheerios, and the girls favorite stuffed animal in their bags. It was hard to leave the house without a ton of things when you had two babies. They each needed things and Jason was going to be out all day. He'd be able to purchase lunch for them at the zoo but I included their fruit and puffs that they loved so that they didn't have a meltdown at lunch.

That would be the last thing that he needed. The girls could be a lot to handle and I didn't want Jason to not be able to calm them down.
I was worried about how this day was going to go so I reminded him that I would have my cell with me all day. I told him that I'd be shopping and able to meet him if need be. He assured me that he would be fine but I still had my doubts.

I gave my girls extra kisses and hugs before buckling them into their car seats in daddy's car. They waved bye bye as Jason pulled out of the drive. I missed them already and it sort of annoyed me. I knew that Jason would do his best to take care of them. He loved his daughters very much. I wished that I trusted him a bit more but it was what it was. I had armed him with everything he would need for the day. With any luck, he wouldn't need all of the things I packed for him but just in case, they were there.

I went back inside and grabbed my keys and purse, then climbed into my SUV and headed out to the stores to do a little shopping. I stopped at the consignment shop first to sell the girls clothes then I dropped by the domestic violence shelter, known as Hope House, to drop off the donations. Up next was my eye doctor appointment where I picked out new glasses. After that was the local department store to find new clothes for the girls. They were growing so fast and now that they were going to be outside more, I wanted to make sure they had pants and shirts, as well as new shoes and socks. I tossed outfits into a cart two at a time, adding undershirts and socks. I found two adorable jackets in complimentary colors and put them into the cart as well.

I was enjoying my time out of the house without the girls. It was so much easier to shop for them without them screaming or wanting to get out of the stroller. Hell, not having to bring a double stroller was nice. I was heading towards the educational toys when I spotted my mother a few aisles over. I really wasn't in the mood for her today so I ducked into an aisle and hurried down the back of the store towards the restrooms hoping I could make it in there quickly and hide out for a minute. I indicated to the attendant that I was going to leave my cart for a few minutes while I ducked into the bathroom.

She nodded that it was fine and I almost ran in and locked myself in a stall. Here I was a grown woman with children, hiding from her mother in a public bathroom. As the minutes ticked by, I was sure the attendant was thinking that I had something majorly wrong with me or that I'd fallen in or something else just as insane. I finally gave up and went back out to shop. I had just sat my purse down in the cart when my mother spotted me.

I looked up to see she had decided to turn around and walk away from me. Had she really just done that knowing full well I could see that she had? I buried my anger and hurt down deep and knew I'd discuss this with Dr. Morales next week.

I glanced down at my phone when it vibrated to find a text from Jason.

'Going well, girls love the flamingos and the bears. About to have lunch. I'll text ya in a bit'

I smiled to myself knowing that my girls were having a fun day. I could only hope I could get back to my nice day after my mother had just pulled that crap. I still couldn't believe it. I probably would have accused someone of lying if I hadn't seen it with my own eyes.

I pushed my buggy along the aisles, looking at the toys, putting a few in the cart and continuing on my way. I had pushed all thoughts of my mother aside because if I didn't, I was going to cause a scene in this store and that wouldn't be good for any of us.

Once I was done shopping for the twins, I headed to the ladies department to get some new clothes for myself. I hadn't had anything new in a while and I was planning on getting at least a part time job so I'd need a few new things. Most of my clothes no longer fit me after having twins. My body wasn't the same petite, thin body it used to be. I had curves in places I'd never had them before. I wasn't overweight by any means but I was certainly heavier than I had been.

If I were truthful I would have admitted that prior to carrying the girls, I was too thin. I worried so much about my weight. I was sure it was a symptom of my anxiety. I felt I needed to be perfect because I was the daughter that hadn't been abused or abducted. I barely ate, determined to keep my slim figure.

Then I was pregnant and everything changed. Jason had always told me he loved my body no matter the shape of it. It didn't matter to him if I carried weight or I was thin. He loved me regardless.

I'd been so speechless and fell even more in love with him then. How had I screwed this all up so badly? How could I have pushed him away the way I had? He had been my entire world and then something changed inside of me and I just had to push him away. I had to push everyone away because they could all hurt my girls. I had wanted to keep them safe and I was the only one who could do that so I pushed everyone out of my life one by one.

It made no more sense to me than it did to anyone else. Somewhere inside of my brain, I'd decided that only I was good for my girls. Man, Dr. Morales was going to wonder what the fuck was going on in our family that both daughters could be so fucked in the head.

It would have been funny if it wasn't so damn scary. Molly had an excuse. She'd been through Hell and survived. I hadn't. My life had been so easy compared to hers. If anyone deserved to have a breakdown, it was Molly.

I had a life most people would kill for. I had a husband who loved me and didn't cheat on me or hit me. I had two beautiful little girls who made every day a new adventure. Those girls had completed my soul. I hadn't even known it was missing something until I saw their little faces for the first time. Of course, they were all covered in that cottage cheese and strawberry jam looking gunk, but still, they were amazing. I had done that. I created that life, nurtured and nourished it. I had given them life from my own body.

By the time I was done shopping, I was more convinced than ever that I was mentally a nut case and that Dr. Morales should lock me up and throw away the key. I also secretly hoped that she wouldn't do either.

I sat in my car, with it running, while I drank a coke and had a Little Debbie snack cake as my lunch. It wasn't healthy or nutritious but damn it was good. And that was exactly what I needed then.

Good.

Hours later, when I was home and had heard all about the girls' and Jason's trip to the zoo and we had all eaten dinner, I was sure that I'd imagined my mother hurrying away from me. I told Jason about it after we put the girls down for the night. He thought that maybe I had mistaken someone else for my mother. He sure didn't think that she'd turn her back on me without speaking to me in public.

I knew that he was wrong. It was her. I had seen her with my own two eyes. I could even still smell her Chanel perfume. I wanted to believe him. I wanted to believe that she wouldn't do that but she had. She had done just that and it hurt me. It was as if she'd plunged a knife into my chest. The pain was no less than that. I wanted to scold her for it. I wanted to hurt her as much as she'd hurt me today in that store.

I convinced myself that she deserved it and so much more. I forced myself to stay calm and not call her and tell her how I felt after that. I wanted to call my father and tell him what she'd done too. Maybe then he'd be on my side instead of her's. He'd chosen her side all those years ago when she let Daisy get taken. Why should now be any different?

Everyone talked about how they were such great parents. But were they really? Didn't they have a daughter get abducted and then years later return only to kill herself in the end? And rumor was they had another daughter, though no one really knew who she was because everyone, including my parents, were focused on Molly and what she needed.

I was forgotten. I was shoved to the side. No one listened to me now or then. I was always sitting on the outside just looking into our family. I think that's why I felt such a strong connection with Molly when I got older. We'd both lost years to being neglected and abused. Only my neglect and abuse was wrapped up in a pretty little package and tied up with a bow. Everyone thought that my life was so grand and full of love and joy.

In reality my childhood was lonely and scary. I was always worried that I'd say the wrong thing and Molly would go crazy. I worried that I'd upset my momma and Daddy said she didn't need anything else to upset her. So I was always the good girl, on my best behavior so that I didn't upset momma. I never really got to be a kid.

Molly's innocence was stolen from her but so was mine. I was every bit as traumatized by Molly's past as Molly was. It affected every aspect of my life. I wasn't allowed to be outside alone, or walk to my friend's house or even to the school bus on my own. I wasn't allowed to sleep over at someone's house because my mother didn't know them well enough or because they had a father who looked a little "off" as momma would say.

Perhaps she thought she was protecting me when in reality she was suffocating me. I never felt like I could breathe in that house. Another reason I spent so much time at Molly's apartment. She gave me the freedom to breathe, to be me and it was glorious. I craved that feeling of freedom so much. I had been sheltered my entire life so one little taste of freedom and I was addicted. It was like a drug, powerful and all consuming.

Molly understood that need. She nurtured it in me. She saw me for the person I was and allowed me to just be her. I wanted nothing more than to live my life and not be told how bad the world was. Molly gave me that. She showed me the bad but she also showed me the good in the world. She showed me that not everyone had bad intentions. I was grateful for that. I wasn't afraid when I was with Molly. I knew that no matter what, she had my back and she would protect me at all costs.

That's why I spent all my time there. Partly to help her, the other part to help myself. Living in her shadow had taken a toll on my life and I had no one that would listen to me when I tried to tell them that I needed more. Momma always sent me away saying she was busy with something for Molly. Daddy was at work or tired. I got lost in the shuffle my whole life.

I was doing my best to not do that to my kids. I didn't want this generational abuse to continue. Because it was abuse, plain and simple. I didn't need Dr. Morales to tell me that. I figured that out on my own years ago.

I once had longed for the perfect family. A family where we ate dinner together every night and talked about our day. A family that went on vacations and enjoyed being with one another. I wanted to be close to my sister. I wanted to be heard, not when I did bad, but all the time. I wanted my presence to be felt and appreciated and it wasn't. I needed someone to hear my screams for attention but no one ever did.

I was sure that Dr. Morales would understand all of this but I couldn't wait any longer. I had to get it out of my system before it destroyed me. I wanted Jason to understand why I had pushed him away. I wanted him to know that my mother wasn't the saint she made herself out to be. She wasn't a good woman or mother. She tried. She had really tried for a while but now, she had given up. After Molly died, she was no longer the mother I'd known my whole life.

She was worse.

She never held her tongue when it came to my life and my mistakes. She reminded me of them daily. And I'd let her. She was my mother after all. And I was a good, dutiful daughter who didn't dare disobey her. To be frank, I was rather tired of being a good daughter. I wanted her to hear me when I told her that I needed things from her. She had always put Molly first and yes, Molly may have needed her more, but I needed her too. I was a child. I needed my mother to guide me, to love me and she didn't. She put all of her energy into Molly.

I was never her priority and apparently I still wasn't. God how I wanted to hate her but I couldn't. In spite of everything, I loved my mother.

⇒*Chapter Twenty-Four*⇐

Jason and the girls arrived home around six o'clock. I'd just finished making dinner when they walked in. The girls were wide awake and full of energy while Jason looked like he hadn't slept in twelve days. I couldn't help but laugh when he dropped the girls' bags on the floor after he put them down. He sat down on the couch and I wasn't sure he would make it up the stairs for bed later.

"Stay there, I'll bring you a plate after I get the girls settled."

"I can come into the kitchen," he said, only half meaning it.

"Nope, you've done enough today." I called out to him from the kitchen.

I sat the girls in their chairs, filled the trays with chicken and noodles along with green beans, and their sippy cups. They were already happily and hungrily eating while I made Jason's plate. I piled it high with food, knowing he most likely hadn't had a chance to eat much all day. I grabbed a beer from the fridge and took it to him in the living room.

"Thank you," he said with a smile. He was eating like he'd been starved for years when I went back to make my own plate to eat with the girls.

I cleaned up the girls and took them up for a bath then got them ready for bed. They'd had a long day and both were rubbing their eyes sleepily. I put their lavender lotion on them to help them sleep soundly and made sure they were warm and had their favorite toys to sleep with.

Once they were settled and sleeping, I headed back down to check on Jason. He was asleep and snoring on the couch. I chuckled to myself and grabbed a blanket from the basket and put it over him. I took his completely clean plate to the kitchen and cleaned up from dinner.

Once the dishwasher was running, I headed back to the living room to grab the girls' bags and then turned off all the lights after double checking the lock on the door and went upstairs. I tossed their bags on the chair in my bedroom, changed into my pjs and climbed into bed to read for a few hours.

I woke up the next morning to find my book open on the bed next to me. I had managed to wake before the girls so I could pee, brush my teeth and maybe even grab a quick shower before they woke.

I was just brushing the knots out of my hair when they started crying. They wanted to get up and eat so I hurried to finish dressing.

I got them dressed as quickly as I could to try to quiet them down but they weren't going to be happy until they had pancakes in front of them. I managed to get them down the stairs without falling and got them set up for breakfast. I'd made pancakes and froze them over the weekend so I just popped them into the microwave for a minute so that they were warm but not too hot for the girls. While they cooled a little, I cut bananas up for them and gave them their milk in a sippy cup.

They were happily eating their pancakes when Jason joined us in the kitchen. He poured himself a cup of coffee and sat down at the table in his usual place. We both watched the girls as we finished our coffee. I poured myself a fresh cup and offered him another. Refusing, he said that he was going to go shower the day before off of him. I wondered if he planned to go into the office that morning or if he was taking another day off.

By the time he made it back down to the living room, the girls were playing in their little fenced off area. Molly was playing with the piano toy she'd gotten last month and Daisy was busy stacking blocks. He wasn't dressed for the office so I assumed he wasn't going in but I didn't ask. I went about my day as normal.

I cleaned the kitchen while the girls played. I enjoyed my routine because it was familiar and I rarely varied from it. Today was no different. Seeing that Jason was still in the living room, I ran upstairs and put a load of laundry in. I quickly made my bed and straightened the girls' room, picking up toys and straightening their crib bedding.

I headed back downstairs and tackled the living room, putting toys away, picking up clothes and socks and tossing them into a basket. I folded up the blanket I'd used for Jason the night before and checked on the girls.

By the time I was done, it was time for story time and I chose a book the girls both loved. Good Night Gorilla was one of their favorites and they always giggled when the gorilla followed the zookeeper home.

We sat and played after the story was done. I put on a puppet show for the girls and sang to them. I glanced over to find Jason watching us.

"You can join, if you'd like."

He smiled and was instantly sitting on the floor with us, playing blocks with Daisy while Molly and I played the piano toy some more. She had far more talent than I did and Jason and I smiled at one another at how smart our daughters were.

We spent the next few hours playing as a family before it was time for lunch. Jason got up to make it, allowing me the extra time with Molly and Daisy. I was the one who usually had to make all of the meals and clean. I rarely had time to sit down and just enjoy time with my girls until the end of the night right before bed.

After a lunch of chicken nuggets, fries and fruit, Jason and I took the girls up for their nap. Both girls fought us every step of the way but eventually settled down and laid down in their cribs.

Jason still looked tired and I suggested he take a nap. It would certainly make it easier for me to grab one while the girls were down. I was tired and I knew that Jason was too.

"A nap sounds good, but I thought that maybe we could talk, or something."

My eyes widened as he closed the distance between us and put his finger under my chin, pressing his lips to mine in a slow and gentle kiss. I leaned into him, not wanting to break this spell we were both under. I had missed the way he kissed me.

Before I knew what was happening, he scooped me up in his arms and carried me to our bedroom. We spent the afternoon making love while the girls slept. It was as if we'd never been apart.

I knew that we were rushing into things but I couldn't stop myself or him, even if I'd wanted to. We were meant to be together and making love with Jason seemed like the best way to spend an afternoon.

We lay together, spent and Jason held me close.

"I love you, Lily."

"I love you too, Jason."

It was the only words we needed. When the girls cried, we both threw on our clothes and went to get them. Being a family was so important to the both of us then. I loved how he helped out with the twins. Jason was a good father and I was lucky to have a man like him in my life. A man who forgave me when I pushed him away and who never stopped loving me even when I didn't deserve it.

We spent the rest of the day enjoying our girls as they played and we lounged together on the couch. Jason ordered dinner in so that I didn't have to cook and I was beyond grateful for that.

After dinner and a bath, the girls went to bed without a fuss. Jason and I raced back to the bedroom and spent the night making love. We had a lot of time to make up for.

⩾Chapter Twenty-Five⩽

The next day, my mother called.

I wasn't sure I wanted to answer her and stared at my ringing phone for quite some time. I decided to not answer but she called back mere seconds later. I snatched my phone off the coffee table and answered it.

"Mom, I'm really not in the mood to talk to you today."

"Is this Lily Anders?", a strange voice asked.

"Who is this?"

"Ma'am, I need to verify that you are indeed Lily Anders."

"Yes, I'm Lily but it's not Anders any more. I'm married. It's Lily Cooper now."

"Mrs. Cooper, my name is Officer Lund. Your mother has been in an accident and you're listed as her emergency contact. She's alive, but she is at Bellevue Memorial Hospital. You may want to come down and see her."
"What happened," I asked a little too calmly. I wasn't even sure I wanted to go to the hospital to see her. My mother drove like a damn snail so she couldn't be that badly hurt.

She was hit by a car as she crossed the street. She's alive, Mrs. Cooper but it doesn't look good. I can send a car to get you if you need one."

"No, no. I have to arrange for a sitter for the girls but I'll be there as soon as possible. Has anyone called my father?"

"No ma'am. You were listed as the emergency contact so we called you first."

"Okay, I'll call him. Better for him to hear it from me. Is she…." I hesitated before continuing. "Is it likely she's going to die?"

"I'm not a doctor Mrs. Cooper but if it were my mother, I'd want to be here rather quickly just in case."

"Okay. I understand. Thank you, for calling."

I called Jason the moment I hung up with the officer. I told him what was happening and asked if he could come home to take care of the girls so I could get to the hospital. He was on his way but I couldn't wait. My neighbor came over to sit with the girls until Jason got home. I hurried to my car and turned towards the hospital.

I called my father from the car, getting his voicemail. I called back multiple times with no answer. I sent a text asking him to call me as soon as he got the message. I told him it was an emergency.

I called a couple of his friends looking for him and one, Tim, seemed to think he was fishing and said he'd go find him for me. I asked him to please not tell him what was happening but just to get him to call me as soon as he could. I thanked Tim and parked my car, running across the parking lot of the emergency room.

I came to an abrupt stop when I hit the door to the ER and security had a check in station set and wouldn't allow me past until I showed my identification and had my temperature taken. I had forgotten how the world had changed since Covid and I was not amused with this entire process. I told him who I was there to see and he typed something into his computer, frowned and then asked me if I was a family member.

"Yes, I'm her daughter." I was doing my best to be nice to this man wearing his little rent-a-cop badge and uniform.

"Okay, you're good to go in. Stop at the desk and someone will take you back."

I rolled my eyes, gathered my purse and keys and hurried over to stand in line at the window. I stayed more than 6 feet from the people in front of me because I sure didn't want to take any germs home to the girls. Once I got to the window, the young lady at the desk held up a finger for me to wait a moment and once again, I did my best to be patient.

"How may I help you?"

She didn't really seem like she wanted to help me but I gave her the benefit of the doubt.

"My mother was brought in. Amy Anders. She was in an accident, they said."

She busied herself with typing something into her computer and frowned, looking back up at me before she spoke.

"Just a moment, ma'am. I'll get someone to take you back to Mrs. Anders."

And just like that, she was gone, disappearing back behind the glass doors that held me in the waiting area while she went to find someone to take me back.

Within minutes a nice young man arrived and escorted me down the maze of halls to my mother's room. He spoke as we walked.

"I want to warn you that she's pretty beat up. It was a very bad accident according to the EMS who brought her in. Right now, she's on a breathing tube because her respirations were very low and we didn't want to take a chance. She's not going to be able to speak to you. She's heavily sedated so she may not know that you're in the room. We do believe that she can hear you, so talk to her if you'd like. The doctor has ordered some tests and one of those is to test her brain function. Dr. Hall will be in shortly to talk to you."

"Thank you," I said, trying to digest everything he'd just told me. "My father should be here soon."

He smiled sadly at me and then stepped aside so I could enter the small room. I tried to prepare myself but nothing could have ever prepared me to see my mother like that. She was pale and looked so fragile and small lying there in that hospital bed, connected to tubes that helped her breathe. She had dried blood in her hair, and smears of blood on her cheek. I wanted to scream for some nurse to come in here and clean her up but I knew that a little blood on her cheek was the least of their worries.

I sat down in the chair beside her bed and put my head in my hands, wondering how I was supposed to prepare my father to see her like this. There was no way I could. No words would make him understand how small and frail she looked. I tried to remember what the nurse or orderly, whomever he was, had told me.

Looking at my mother, I could see that she was in bad shape. I reached out and brushed the hair from her face, speaking softly.

"Oh, Momma, what happened? I don't know if you can hear me, but I love you, Momma. I'm sorry for all the bullshit that's been going on. Daddy's on his way. Tim went to get him from the lake. It's the only place we can figure he is at. Just hang on until he's here, Momma."

I didn't want to think of the worst case scenario but it was staring me in the face every time I looked at my mother lying there in that bed. The fact that she wasn't breathing on her own really worried me. I couldn't lose her. We hadn't made up and gotten past this horrible place we were in. My girls needed her in their life to teach them things I couldn't. It scared me to think about her not making it out of this hospital.

Of course, I'd thought about losing my mother in the last few years. She was getting up there in age and so was my father. They'd both pre-planned their funerals and final arrangements but I hadn't wanted to hear it all at the time. I didn't want to think of them dying, no matter how old they were getting.

Molly's death had made them think about their own mortality and it was awful. They spent months and months talking about all of their plans. Now here I was, sitting next to my mother in a hospital, trying to remember all the crap she wanted at her funeral. I couldn't remember a single thing she'd said. I was sure it was written down in some notebook she had at home. She had everything written down.

I tried my best to shake the thoughts from my mind and focus instead on the woman laying in the bed in front of me. She was breathing thanks to a machine and I worried as the day got later that my dad wasn't going to make it here in time. I tried to call Tim and my father but neither answered.

I sat for a moment, then I called Jason. He answered on the first ring and that told me that he'd been waiting for my call.

"Lily, how is she?"

"She's not awake and looks really bad, Jason. They have her on a breathing machine and said that the doctor has added more tests and once they are done, he will come in and talk to us."

"How is your dad holding up?"

"I don't know. He isn't here yet. I can't get a hold of him or his friend Tim, who went out to the lake to bring Daddy in."

"Take a breath, babe. He will make it in time. How are you doing?"

"I honestly do not know, Jason. She doesn't look good. I don't know if she's only alive because of the machines or if she's still in there somewhere."

"Until you know any difference, she's in there, Lily. Just believe that."

"I'm trying. She never forgave me, you know. She may very well go to her grave hating me. I thought I had more time to make things right."

"You can not think like this. You have to hold it together, babe. Your Dad is going to need you to hold it together for him when he gets there. Give me Tim's number and I can try to call him for you."

I gave him the number I had for Tim and he promised to call me the minute he reached him. Time seemed to be moving in slow motion while I waited for someone to come take my mother for tests and for my father to arrive.

A nurse came in and seemed shocked to find me in the room. "Oh my goodness, no one told me that you were back here."

"I'm her daughter," I said.

"Well it's good she has you here. My name is Teresa and I'm the nurse on duty right now taking care of your mother. I'm going to take her vitals and check her reflexes. They will be coming to take her down for a brain scan and MRI soon. They're a little backed up due to a major accident we had earlier. She's on STAT orders so they will get to her as soon as possible."

"Has there been any improvement since she was brought in?" I needed to know.

She tapped a few things on the computer then looked at me seriously. "No, there hasn't. I'm sorry."

"Is she going to die?"

"I don't know. I can tell you that the doctor that she has is the best brain surgeon in the world and he has been attending since she was brought in. The paramedics in the field knew she had a major head injury so we brought Dr. King in immediately."

"Thank you for being honest and for getting the best doctor for her."

"I'm well aware that this is a very, very hard thing to be dealing with but I do have a few questions I need to ask."

"It's okay, I'll answer to the best of my ability."

"Does your mother have a living will or a DNR?"

"Not that I'm aware of. My father would know. He should be here soon."

"That's good. I hate to say this the way it is going to sound but I don't mean it in a bad way. Think about organ donation. Typically with head injuries, the rest of the organs are in great shape and can help multiple people live."

"I'll keep it in mind." I thanked whoever it was that gave me the ability to turn off my emotions in times of stress.

Teresa finished checking on my mother and making her notes then let me know she'd check on those tests and try to move them along for me. I was still sitting there thinking about what she'd said to me when my dad came rushing in with an orderly trailing behind him trying to get him to stop running.

He glanced over at me then took his place at my mother's bedside before he spoke.

"How is she? What is the doctor saying?"

"She's exactly the same as when I got here. They are waiting on tests before the doctor comes in to talk to us. She's not breathing on her own and they've asked if she has a living will or a DNR in place."

"She does have a living will. It should be on file here. She didn't want to be hooked up to machines. She wanted to be allowed to die if it was her time to go."

He looked over at me and shook his head. He knew my question and he was letting me know that he wouldn't allow them to take her off the machines if there was any chance that she would be okay. I exhaled slowly, thankful that he knew what I needed to know.

We remained in silence for about an hour before I told my father that I was going to go find a chair for him and get us both some coffee. I knew that they weren't going to let us go with her for the tests and they'd make us leave the room if they planned to do them in her room. I wasn't going to miss anything important.

⩾*Chapter Twenty-Six*⩽

I stopped at the nurses station and asked if they could take an extra chair in for my dad and perhaps a pitcher of water or something since it looked like we were going to be here for the night. After that I popped off to the small coffee bar I knew they had in the lobby and got two large coffees, sugar and cream, along with a couple of pastries.

I doubted that they'd get eaten but it was going to be a long night and at some point we were both going to need to eat something. Coffee wasn't going to sustain us unfortunately. I hurried back to the emergency department and followed the nurse back to my mother's room. Daddy was sitting in a chair holding momma's hand.

For the first time I saw him as the old man he'd become. His hair was more gray than black now and he was thin. He was much thinner than I remembered him being. When had my father gotten old?

I handed him the coffee and sat the bag of pastries on the table then went back to my seat. We'd been waiting for far too many hours now and I was about to lose my patience when they came in to do whatever testing the dr wanted. There was a team of people since she was hooked to machines that were breathing for her and I wondered how they were going to get the scans they needed.

Before I knew what was happening, Daddy and I were being ushered out into the hall and huge machines were being wheeled into the small room. We heard the dull conversations and the whirring of the machines as they did whatever it was the doctor wanted to see. We stood out there in that hall, holding our coffee and waited.

Even when they were done with all the action in the room, we still knew nothing more. We now had to wait for the test results and for the doctor to come in to talk to us.

The silence in the room was deafening. My father and I didn't say a word to one another. This wasn't the time or place for us to work things out. Right now we need to support one another and be here for my mother.

I must have fallen asleep at some point because I woke to my father shaking me gently.

"Lily, wake up. Lily," he said quietly.

I opened my eyes, my head pounding. It took a few moments before I remembered where I was. "I'm up," I said groggily.

"The nurse just came in and said the doctor is on the way. He should be here in the next 20 minutes or so."

He handed me a cup of coffee in a styrofoam cup with a lid and filled me in when I raised an eyebrow. "The nurse brought us both a cup. She said it's trash, tastes like mud, and came from the nurses' break room."

"Should be good then." I took a sip, and tried to not make a face at how strong it was. It was coffee at the very least and for that I was thankful. I quickly sent a text to Jason and tried to ignore the need to pee but it became too necessary and I excused myself to hurry to the bathroom just down the hall.

I had just made it back to my mother's cubicle room and sat down when a very striking man in a white coat rushed in. He introduced himself to my father and me then looked over my mother's chart, pulling up pictures of her brain that had multiple colors and some that were just gray, like a normal x-ray.

He left open the images with the colors. He pointed to an area where there was no color. "This signifies that there is no brain activity. Mrs. Anders suffered a traumatic brain injury in the accident. We've seen no brain activity in her frontal lobe at all since she arrived hours ago. I wanted to run these tests to give her body a chance to start to heal but with a brain injury, time often doesn't heal anything. On top of the brain injury, she has a broken collar bone, fractured vertebrae, a broken leg, shattered kneecap, and it appears she's lacerated her liver."

"What does all of that mean, Doctor?" I had to know. Nothing he said really told me anything at all.

"It can mean several things but what I'm seeing on her scans isn't good. I'd be shocked if she ever woke from the coma she's in right now."

"But is it possible?" My father's voice was trembling.

"I know this is hard to hear, Mr. Anders, but the probability of her waking up is less than one percent."

"Doctor, what do we do now? My father needs to know his options so we can make the right decision for him and my mother."

"Well, we can leave her on the machines and transfer her to the ICU but she won't get better. You'll be spending a fortune for many years to come. We can keep her alive, if that's what you want, but she won't have any quality of life at all. Or, the most humane thing to do would be to remove her from life support and let her pass on her own."

"Most humane?" My father's voice was raised and echoed in the room around me. "She's not a dog. She's my wife. Her name is Amy. She is a good woman who has lived a god fearing life, raised two daughters, buried one of them, and generally didn't have an easy life. Show her some respect."

Doctor King looked shaken and honestly, I wouldn't have stopped my dad had he tried to deck him. "I'm sorry Mr. Anders, I didn't mean it to sound heartless. I was just giving you the options. Of course it's a hard decision to make. I wouldn't want to have to make it."

"What is the best case scenario, Doctor?" I was surprised to hear my own voice asking the question.

"If a miracle happens, she will wake up. In my professional opinion, she's not going to. I've seen hundreds of cases like this. Her brain isn't registering pain or feeling. It's simply as if it's shut down and there is no power button to restart it. I wish I had better news for you folks. We can give her a few days, see if the swelling goes down and maybe, if you believe in prayer, God will hear you and she will wake up and go home with you."

"Do you think that is going to happen in her case?" It was me again, how the hell did I ask these things when I was completely lost right this second?

"No, I do not. I think that in a week, she's going to be the same as she is right now, but I am not God. I do not know the miracles He can perform."

"Well, for now, let's give her a week," I said, looking over at my father. He was bent over my mother, smoothing her hair out of her eyes, talking quietly to her. "Daddy, are you okay with that for now?"

"For now," he said without looking up.

Doctor King nodded and let me know that he'd put in the transfer to ICU and that one of the nurses would come in and fill us in on how visitation worked up there. Once we were moved up and I knew her room, I would run to their house and get my father whatever he needed. I knew that he wasn't going to leave her side no matter what happened. He would need things like his toothbrush, clean clothes, his glasses and maybe a book. He could read to Momma. Maybe that would help.

"Daddy, can you come sit beside me for a minute?"

Once he took his place in the chair next to me, I took his hand in mine and filled him in on how Momma was going to ICU and that visitation would be limited. I also let him know that I was going to go pick up necessities for him once she was settled in upstairs. I'd bring him back some food and whatever else he wanted me to bring.

He spoke softly when he did speak but mainly he looked frail and lost. I could see how scared he was. They'd been together for so many years and I knew that he loved her deeply. He got back up and went to sit back at her bedside, taking her hand in his.

Three hours later we were finally upstairs in the ICU. I made sure Dad was settled and spoke with the nurses about keeping an eye on him. I let them know I'd be going home to pick up some things for him then returning.

As I suspected, only one of us could be in the room with her and obviously it was going to be Daddy. I drove to their house, concerned that it was so dark out and that I'd left Jason for so long with the girls. I called him just to check on them. I didn't even realize the time and I woke him.

He mumbled something about the girls being fussy and how they'd just finally settled down for the night. I told him I loved him and that I'd see him in the morning. I turned the music up in the car to keep myself awake.

I hurried into my childhood home as soon as I arrived, locking the door behind me out of habit. Momma never liked the door to be unlocked. I think it stemmed from the whole Molly incident but I wasn't sure. I quickly gathered Daddy's things and grabbed a nightgown for Momma as well as her brush. She would be embarrassed if she could see how knotted her hair was right now.

I packed it all into an overnight bag then went to the kitchen to pack some snacks for Daddy. Crackers, jerky, peanut butter, nuts and more found their way into the bag. I stopped in the living room on my way out to look around. There were photos of Molly and I everywhere with photos of the kids tucked in as well. I picked up a photo of Molly and I when we were little and started to cry.

The tears fell unchecked. I had been through so much in the last few weeks that my emotions and exhaustion finally caught up with me and I lost it right there in my parents' living room.

"Fuck, I need you right now, Molly. I don't know how to do this. Losing you was so hard and now Momma. I'm not sure that I can do this. I will have to be strong for Daddy and take care of arrangements. How do I do that all alone? Why did you have to leave me alone here to take care of them as they got older?"

I was angry, angrier than I'd ever been. I was angry with God and the Universe or whoever the fuck was in charge of the shit that happens here on Earth. My mother wasn't innocent or even the best mother in the world, but she wasn't a bad woman. She'd lived through Hell and never gave up hope or faith. She didn't deserve any of what was happening to her. She shouldn't be lying in a hospital bed on life support.

Daddy didn't deserve this either. He shouldn't be facing the toughest decision of his life. He'd already lost my sister, given his entire life to not giving up on finding her, and he never let my mother forget that she was loved. Their love story was eternal and I wasn't sure that my father would survive a single night without my mother.

This wasn't something either of them imagined happening. I wasn't sure they'd even spent a night apart in all the years they'd been together. Daddy may have slept on the couch a time or two but they hadn't spent a night where they weren't under the same roof. Even when they were fighting, Daddy loved my mother beyond all others.

He took her side no matter what. He took her side against me, Molly, his mother, her mother, everyone. It was unconditional love between them. I truly hoped that my mother could feel that love even now. She deserved that.

How was Daddy going to survive without her? Would he stay in their home? Would he survive her death? I had no idea what the answers were or how we were going to get through this but I knew that no matter what, Daddy was going to need help.

I would have to be there for him, not that I even had any other thoughts at the moment. I knew that Jason would step up and help out as well but it was going to be tough on all of us. Momma was the center of Daddy's world and with her gone, he was going to lose his mind.

I pulled myself out of my thoughts, picked up all of the things I'd packed for him and Momma and headed out the door. I left the kitchen light on because I couldn't bear to leave the house dark. I whispered a silent prayer as I locked the door behind me and climbed into my car.

Chapter Twenty-Seven

Back at the hospital, the nurses allowed me into the room with Daddy as long as I promised to just drop off his stuff and leave.

"Hey, Daddy, I brought you some clothes and snacks." I was already putting things out for him so that it would be easier for him when he wanted to rest. "The nurses are going to have a chair brought in for you that will recline and will fold out into a small bed type of situation. I'm sure it's not comfortable at all but it's better than sleeping while sitting up."

"Thank you," he said without looking up.

"You're welcome, Daddy. I brought Momma some things as well. I thought you could brush her hair and maybe the nurses could help you change her into her own pajamas."

"That's nice, Lily."

"Daddy, please eat something and maybe get some rest. I can't stay. The nurses gave me 10 minutes and that was 15 minutes ago. I'll be out in the waiting room just outside the door to the unit. If you need me, a nurse will come get me."

I was about to walk out of the room when my father stopped me with a hand on my arm. "Thank you, Lily. For being here, for picking up all of this stuff."

He hugged me tightly and I saw for the first time that my father was far older now than I remembered. He was frail and old now. I hugged him back, holding on a little longer than necessary.

"You're welcome, Daddy."

He went back to his chair and I headed out to the waiting room. As soon as I sat down, I called Jason.

"Hey," he answered, the house quiet. "How's your mom?"

"No change. I ran to the house and picked up clothes for Daddy for a few days and a bunch of snacks. The nurses said they'll make sure he gets meals, etc, but I can't leave him here alone."

"I'm sure he appreciates everything you're doing, babe."

"He hugged me, Jason. He hasn't done that in years."

"That's a good thing, isn't it?"

"I guess. He just looks so old and frail now. I don't know if he will survive losing her."

"The doctors still have no hope that she will recover?"

"It's not looking good. The nurse said that her vitals are all exactly the same. They will do another brain scan in a couple of days to allow for swelling to go down and other stuff that didn't make a lot of sense to me."

"You just have to trust that they will do what is right for her. Your father isn't going to be able to do this alone. You do whatever you need to do. The girls and I are fine. I'll bring them by tomorrow to see you and I'll bring you some clothes as well. Anything else you need?"

"You. My babies."

"We aren't going anywhere, Lily. We're right here."

"Thank you," I said softly. We talked about the girls and how their day had gone after I left. The conversation was easy and he told me he loved me before we disconnected.

I realized then that I was lucky. I'd pushed him away, kept him at arm's length, and he still loved me. After everything I'd put him through, he loved me and he was there for me when I needed him.

I squirmed around in the chair until I found a semi comfortable position and laid my head down on my arm. My eyes closed involuntarily. I slept, not well, but I slept. I woke to a code blue in one of the ICU rooms and listened very closely, happy that it wasn't my mother's room.

I hated that some other family was having to deal with what was going on in that room. I said a silent prayer for whomever it was. I got to my feet and went in search of coffee, frowning when I saw that it was 2:00 a.m. It's no myth that no one gets any sleep in the hospital.

The cafeteria was closed, obviously, but I found a vending machine that made what they called coffee. I scanned my card, chose regular coffee, pushed the buttons to add sugar and cream and closed the little door when the machine told me to. I waited for the coffee to brew. At least it smelled good. When the machine beeped at me again, I opened the little door and took out my steaming cup which now had a lid on it.

The coffee cup was very hot on my hand but it didn't matter. The coffee was bitter and tasted more like dark water than actual coffee. I choked it down, and made my way back to my spot in the waiting room.

One of the nurses came out to check on me and offered me a blanket and pillow. She explained that the hospital did have a couple of family rooms on the unit but that right now the father of an eight year old girl was in one so that he and mom could alternate sitting with her so she wouldn't be alone if she woke up. The other room was occupied by the family of a young man in his teens who had been in a horrible tractor accident.

Together we prayed for them and Momma. She said as soon as a room opened, she'd let me know and I thanked her. She said she would check on Daddy and let him know that I was still out here in case he needed anything.

When she was gone, I settled in with a book I'd found in the gift shop. It wasn't something that I'd normally read but it kept me from going completely stir crazy out here in the waiting room. So far, I was the only one out here. I guess most people in ICU didn't get many visitors since things were so limited.

I don't know when I fell asleep but I woke to find Jason and the girls playing on the floor. I smiled and got down with them to play. Daisy crawled right into my lap and we played with her blocks. I looked over her head and mouthed 'thank you' to Jason, who smiled back at me while playing balls with Molly.

The girls did amazingly well and my father even came out to the waiting room to see them and sit with us for a little while. He seemed a little more relaxed than he had been earlier in the morning when I'd checked on him. I wondered if he was starting to accept that Momma may not ever come out of the coma. It would be for the best if he could accept it sooner rather than later.
He played with the girls and even came down to the cafeteria with us to have ice cream with the girls. The girls loved their Poppy and he was so good with them. They would be what would get him through his grief. These girls he loved, my girls.

After Daddy went back to the ICU, Jason and I took the girls outside and walked around the hospital. It wasn't ideal but it gave us time together and I thanked him again for bringing them by. I didn't want to leave my dad alone here and I knew that Jason was making a big sacrifice for me so that I could stay.

We talked about the girls' routine and how best for him to make sure they didn't overrun him the next few days. He mentioned that he'd taken a week off of work to give my dad and I time to figure things out. The girls squealed and "talked" up a storm while we walked. They loved to be outside and Jason promised to take them out more when they got home.

I kissed them all goodbye and helped Jason strap the girls into their car seats. I stood in the parking lot waving at them long after I lost sight of the car. I hated being away from the girls but they were safe and taken care of. Daddy needed me now and so did Momma and no matter what had happened before, I was going to be here for them.

I decided to continue my walk instead of going back inside right away. I wanted a chance to talk to Molly.

"Molly, I know you're somewhere watching all of this. Can you please do something to make this easier on Daddy? And if you could maybe keep an eye on Momma while she's out, I'd appreciate it. She kinda needs you now more than ever and I'm betting that by now you have some pull up there. Yes, I said UP there. If anyone deserves to live in paradise for the afterlife, it's you, Moll. It's the absolute least that the Universe could do for you after what it put you through. God, I wish you were here. I just want to talk to you, to have you hold my hand while we wait for Daddy to come out and tell us what's happening. At least with you here, I'd have a friend who understands why I feel so guilty that she's lying there and the last thing she said to me was that she didn't forgive me."

I really did wish she was here to talk to. She would understand where I was inside my head and why I was that way right now. She was the only one who could understand how complicated life with our mother was and could be. I needed a friend like her in my corner right now. She'd have been right here next to me, driving the nurses insane with her constant questions and demands. With her here, Daddy would have had someone else to focus on instead of what was happening in that room with Momma.

Unfortunately, Molly wasn't here and I was stuck all alone waiting on news from doctors on whether my mother was going to come out of this coma and be her old self again. It sucked not having my sister around and I was angrier than I'd ever been with Jim and Diane. They'd stolen her from us all and even though we'd gotten her back, she wasn't whole thanks to them.

Chapter Twenty-Eight

I headed back in to see if Daddy needed anything before I settled back into my spot in the waiting area. The nurses let me know that the doctor had ordered some more tests for today and I thanked them for keeping me updated on what was going on with my mother's care. I knocked softly on the door to Momma's room in case Daddy was sleeping. I found him sitting next to her bed, holding her hand, his head on the bed and snoring softly. I tiptoed around the room, pressed a light kiss to Momma's forehead and headed back out. I'd send him a text in a bit, but for the time being he needed to sleep. This wasn't easy on him at all and with the tests happening he was going to need all the sleep he could get now.

I settled back into my chair in the waiting area and picked up the book I'd started reading earlier. It really wasn't that interesting at all but it killed the time. I was about four chapters in when Daddy came out and said that they'd come to get Momma for tests and asked if I'd like to join him in the cafeteria.

I smiled and said of course. We both chose tea and a salad for a late lunch and ate in silence for a while. When we did speak, we talked about the girls and anything that avoided conversation about what was going on with Momma.

"She's gone."

He said it so quietly that I wasn't sure I'd even heard it. I looked up from my lunch and nodded at him. I had no idea what to say to him to make it any easier.

"I'm sorry, Daddy. I wish that I could change it for you."

"She never wanted to live on machines and I'm being selfish because I'm not ready to let her go just yet. She is probably so mad at me."

I reached out and covered his hand with mine and squeezed gently. "She's not mad at you. She understands that you love her and how hard this must be for you."

"She most certainly doesn't understand. I can promise you that. But…..I have to make peace with the fact that she's gone. I know when they come in to tell me about the results of her test I'm going to have a big decision to make and I don't want to make the wrong one. I'm just not ready to let her go yet, Lily."

"I understand. I truly do. You've already lost so much but you have to listen to what the doctors say first, Daddy. Maybe there is some hope that she can come out of this just fine."

He shook his head and wiped the tears from his eyes. I wanted to give him hope but I knew that it didn't look good for her. The swelling on her brain had to have gone down by now and she should have woken up if she was going to do so at all. Each day that passed with her still in a coma was one day closer to having to make the decision to remove her from life support.

My mother was a stubborn woman, had been all of her life. I was sure she was fighting to come back to my father but this may be a battle she couldn't win. I'd been praying so hard for her to wake up but it seemed that the harder I prayed, the further from waking up she got. Maybe it was just her time to go.

"I don't know how I'm going to do this, Lily. How do I let her go?"
I held his hand and let him cry before I spoke, partly because I needed to gather myself so I could be strong for him.

"I wish I had words to make it easier for you. I wish I could say something like letting her go is the only option but we both know that things aren't always so cut and dry. You have to just do what you feel she would want and then live with that decision. The only guarantee I can give you, Daddy, is that you won't be alone. Jason and I are here for you. We love you and we will help you in any way that we can."

"I know and I appreciate that more than you could ever know."

We finished our lunch in silence, both of us understanding the gravity of the situation that we faced when we returned to the ICU. The doctor had warned us that the chances of her waking were slim to none but Daddy had wanted to give her a chance. Now that he'd sat with her for a few days, he understood that the shell of a body that lay in that hospital bed wasn't his wife and may never be again. What made her Amy was gone. Everything he loved about his wife was no longer there and he had to find a way to accept that reality. I wish I could have helped him figure that all out but I was dealing with my own feelings around my mother's impending death.

We'd still been in the midst of a fight, with her having decided to not forgive me yet, when the accident happened. Now I may never have the chance to make things right with her and I wasn't really sure I was going to be able to handle that. I was still trying to figure out how I was going to deal with my own emotions while trying to help my father with all of the necessary arrangements and his own feelings over everything that was happening now.

I knew that Jason would be there to help with everything but I wasn't sure how much I could lay at his feet. He was already overburdened with the twins and with the two of us trying to figure out our own marriage.

I tried to not think about what was sure to be the hardest goodbye of my life so far. We stepped off the elevator and I hugged my father, reassuring him that he was strong enough to face anything and that I'd be here for him every step of the way. He promised to come get me the moment the doctors had news and I settled back into my seat, watching him walk back into the unit where my mother was.

Chapter Twenty-Nine

The days blended together while I was here. I was beyond tired at this point and ready to go home and shower in my own bathroom and sleep in my own bed. I wanted to wake up and see my girls, feed them breakfast, take them for a walk or something. Anything would have been better than being stuck here in this damn chair waiting to find out if my mother was going to ever wake up again.

Complaining wasn't going to help but I needed to let some of these emotions out before I exploded. I called Jason and checked in with him. Daisy wasn't feeling well and it worried me but Jason said that he'd given her the medication that the doctor suggested and if she wasn't better in 24 hours he would take her in to be seen. I was impressed that he had handled her being sick so well and I told him so.

He did his best to distract me by talking about everything except my mother. He did a darn good job too. At the end of the call I told him about my lunch with my father and what he'd said. Jason was sympathetic of course, but I could tell that he wanted me home and I wanted to be there just as badly.

This would soon pass and life would go back to some semblance of normalcy but it would never truly be the same. Daddy was going to have to learn to live without Momma and so was I. The girls most likely wouldn't even remember her and she would only exist for them in the videos on my phone.

I hated the thought that my girls wouldn't know her or Molly. They would never have the chance to love either of them and it broke my heart.

I was still thinking about it when the nurse appeared and asked me to step into my mother's room. Doctor Lund was a few moments behind her and Daddy and I sat waiting to hear the news, be it good or bad.

"Just as we suspected, she has no brain activity. I'm sorry that the news isn't better but the swelling has gone down significantly and we are seeing no brain waves on any of her scans."

"What are our options?" My father was holding it together the best that he could.

"We can keep her on support and allow her to fully heal but I don't think that is going to change very much. The other option is to remove the support and allow her to pass naturally."

"How long after removing the support would that happen?" I was surprised to hear myself ask the question but I needed to know.

"It could take an hour or it could take a couple of days. There really is no way of knowing, especially given the condition she is in. I know that it's a hard decision to face but we are here to support you in your choice. There is no pressure to decide today. Take all of the time you need. In the meantime, we will continue to monitor her vitals and brain activity. Should anything change, we would notify you immediately."

"Thank you. It is a lot to have to process," my father said quietly.

"I'm sorry I don't have better news for you Mr. Anders. If you need anything at all just have the nurse call me."

And with that he was gone and we were left to make the hard decisions. I asked Daddy if he wanted me to stay with him for a while and he nodded. We sat quietly, both of us lost in thought, both trying to figure out what to do.

A few hours passed without either of us speaking and the nurses coming and going, monitoring Momma's vitals and checking on us. They were breaking the rules by allowing us both to stay in the room but they looked the other way given the news we'd received. The nurses here were compassionate and kind and I appreciated it more than they'd ever know. They took very good care of my mother for us and I was eternally grateful for that. They also made sure that my father was comfortable and that he ate every single day.

Being on the ICU floor meant that something traumatic had happened to someone you loved and these nurses just understood that sometimes it meant you were going to be emotional and maybe not so nice to them. They took it all in stride and never had a cross word for anyone. They did their very best to care for their patients and their loved ones.

I made a note to send them lunch one day soon. They deserved it and it was the very least that I could do to thank them.

I continued to sit with my parents the rest of the day, soaking up the time with Momma and helping Daddy with anything he needed. By the time dinner rolled around, Daddy was ready to escape the room. He said that it felt like it was closing in on him.

We decided to leave the hospital for our meal and Daddy chose a little diner just around the corner. The nurses had promised to call my cell if anything at all changed while we were gone. I doubted that we'd get a call but it made Daddy feel better so we made sure the service was good and my phone was charged.

We both ordered chicken and dumplings, veggies and potatoes and I was looking forward to this meal. It was the first real food that we'd had since Momma had the accident. We sat quietly waiting for our food. I wondered if he'd made a decision but I didn't want to ask.

Asking meant that I would find out if my mother would soon pass on or if he'd allow her to live in the state that she was in. I couldn't figure out what would be worse and a part of me truly did not want to know what choice he'd made. He would tell me when he was ready and I wasn't going to pressure him into a decision.

This was hard enough on him and I wanted him to know that I supported him no matter what. And so, we sat in silence yet again. It had become the norm for us since being at the hospital. I really didn't want to get used to this. I thought about how life would change with either choice he made.

If he chose to keep her on the machines, it would be daily visits to make sure she was okay until we could figure out where she would go to continue this "life". I had no concept of how to begin to figure that all out. It would be me. I was the one that would have to figure it out because Daddy wasn't going to be able to take care of it.

He would be beside himself just trying to figure out how he was going to survive and pay for all of this. It would be extremely expensive to keep her alive. Not to mention that she really wouldn't still be alive in any sense of the word.

Should he choose to let her pass peacefully, I would be left to handle the funeral arrangements. I would have to be strong and help him deal with it all, while my own grief was put on hold. Letting her go, that was the only correct choice in my opinion but it wasn't my decision to make.
After we ate, Daddy asked me to take the long way back. He sat quietly beside me in the car for several long minutes before he spoke.

"I'm letting her go, Lily. It's what she would want me to do. She would want to be able to be with Daisy now. This is just her body here, not her spirit. She deserves the respect and love I can give her by letting her go."

I took a deep breath before I spoke. "I think you're doing the right thing, Daddy. Like you said, she's not here, this is just her body. The things that made her Momma are gone. I know this isn't easy on you. I know that you've had to make hard decisions for her and for yourself. I want you to know that I'm not going anywhere, no matter what. I'm here to support and love you through this."

"I appreciate that. I don't know how to manage this world without your mother. She was the glue that held it all together."

"I know, Daddy. I can't imagine how hard this is for you to do. I also know that Momma would be proud of you for making the choice she would want. She counted on you her entire adult life to keep her safe and make her happy. You've done an amazing job of that. You gave her two daughters, a lifetime of happiness, and you. She had everything she could have ever wanted out of life."

"Thank you, Lily. She gave me just as much happiness in this life we spent together. She was my entire world."

There was nothing more that needed to be said. He'd said everything in those few sentences and my heart broke for this strong man that I'd looked up to my entire life. He had loved my mother but he'd also respected her and liked her. They were best friends and they had gotten through the hardest things any parent could get through together. I knew that making this decision was the worst for him but he understood that this woman he'd loved his whole life was no longer here with us even if her body still was.

I held back my tears because I was sure that seeing my father break down would be the last thing that I could handle now. I would wait until I was alone in the bathroom at the hospital before I gave in to the grief that was tearing me apart.

Chapter Thirty

An hour later, I sat in the bathroom in the lobby and sobbed. My body shook and I just couldn't seem to stop. Daddy was waiting for me upstairs but I needed to take the time to let it out if I planned on making it home tonight. The next few hours were going to be hard, harder than I'd had to deal with since Molly died and I needed every ounce of strength I could muster up. So I sat on the floor of a bathroom just off the lobby and I cried.

I cried for my mother and all the words that weren't said. I cried for how much I wanted her to wake up so I could tell her that I forgave her and loved her. I wanted her to love me back.

The next days passed by in a blur and I couldn't even tell you how we made it through. Daddy came home to stay with us. The girls loved having Grandpa there and I think they helped him survive the days. I heard him crying at night and my heart shattered with each sob that escaped him. Jason did his best to help my father through this. He went to the funeral home with me to make the arrangements. Daddy just couldn't do it and I stepped up. It was my place to take care of this for my mother.

The funeral would be small, not because she didn't have a ton of friends but because I wasn't about to put my father through something huge. He was barely hanging on and too many people would send him over the edge.

I chose a pale pink coffin for her that matched the one we'd buried Molly in. She was to be laid to rest right next to my sister and I knew that would have made them both happy. I spent days ordering flowers and food and making sure that my mother would have a proper home going.

My father spent his days on the verge of tears, hugging my girls every chance he could. He was losing weight and it seemed as if the entire world rested on his shoulders.

For the first time in my adult life, I noticed just how old my father looked. He looked far older than he was and I knew that the last few months had been hard on him. Now he had to lay his wife to rest and it was not going to be easy.

My father had stood beside my mother in the worst of times. When Daisy was missing, he never let the outside world see the rift in their marriage. They'd struggled to stay together. Losing a child can tear a family to shreds but Daddy never left Momma's side.

He'd once told me that he'd made vows that said for better or worse and he honored those vows through the absolute worst that life had given him. When Molly came home, Daddy did his best to ensure that she was loved and safe. He didn't know how to help her with what she'd gone through so he simply was there for her. He never let her forget that he loved her and that he was there when she was ready.

I know that losing my sister had nearly destroyed him. Her death took us all by storm. It was as if a tornado had blown in and twisted our very souls. Molly had that effect on people. She was a natural disaster but man did my father love her.

For a long time I'd resented the way he treated her. I felt that in his eyes Molly could do no wrong, but I was mistaken. He accepted her faults and he looked beyond her behavior because he knew the trauma she'd survived. It took me a very long time to understand all that she'd been through and even now I'm not convinced that I even understand a quarter of it.

Daddy once told me that what Molly had lived through would have killed anyone else, that she was strong and she had a will to survive. The pride in his eyes had been unmistakeable.

I knew that he'd have traded places with her if he could have back then. He'd have saved her from all the pain if she'd have let him. But the pain wasn't his to endure and he knew that. He had understood that Molly existed to protect Daisy and he didn't care which daughter was there, as long as they were home. It was all he had ever wanted.

⪴*Chapter Thirty-One*⪵

Mom's funeral went off without a hitch. Daddy lingered at the church, talking to the pastor while everyone else made their way to the processional. Mom's coffin was loaded into the hearse and we filed into line behind it for her last ride.

I don't remember much about the graveside service. I was busy holding on to my father while Jason held onto our girls. Daddy clung to me, and the program we'd printed up. I could feel his grief while trying to suppress my own.

The service seemed to be over before I could shed a tear and at the same time felt like an eternity. We weren't allowed to stay for them to lower her down but Daddy made me promise we'd be back.

The next few hours were filled with familiar faces expressing their sorrow at our loss. I thanked them all, not even sure of who I was speaking with. My eyes were always scanning the room looking for my father. I found Jason with him more often than not.

My father held onto the coffee cup in his hand as if his very life depended on it and I instantly flashed back to my mother doing the same when Molly died. It was the way they coped when surrounded by people on the worst day of their lives.

I'd known all of my life that Daisy/Molly was the important one but it hadn't actually hurt me until I saw how my father reacted to my mother's death. In that one moment, I knew that it wouldn't have mattered how hard I tried or how perfect I was, Daisy/Molly would always win and be the most important person to them. They'd lost her once and they were trying to make up for that for the rest of the time she'd been alive.

I push the thought from my head and make my way across the room to rescue my father from a distant relative who seems to have cornered him. I smile up at him as I place a hand on his arm. It doesn't matter if Daisy/Molly was the favorite, or needed them the most, I'm the one here and for now, that's all that matters.

⇒Epilogue⇐

As I sit here under the tree, my hand on my sister's gravestone, I wonder if she knew just how much we'd all sacrificed for her. Thoughts ran through my head that I often didn't allow myself to think. At times I'd hated her and other times, I'd have given my life to see her happy and safe. Yet, I always came back here to her. She was the sun and our family revolved around her.

"Daddy is living with us now," I said, trying to not feel angry with her. "We moved to a house with a guest house in the backyard so that he can have his privacy and escape the girls but I don't think he wants to escape them. With Mom being gone for over a year now, he's learned to manage his day to day life without her but I still see the tears in his eyes from time to time. He still loves her just the same as the day he met her. He reminds us of that every morning when he takes his walk to the cemetery to visit with her."

I look around at all the graves and smile when I notice that Molly's and Mom's have the most flowers and I'm the only one here visiting. To me, it means that they are loved and not forgotten. They are both such large parts of our family still.

"Jason and I are still in therapy, working through our issues and challenges but we are happy together. I've had to work on myself a lot to get here but life isn't always easy I guess. The girls are growing so fast, both of them run all the time. Daisy is such a tomboy, always wanting to play in the mud and has already gotten stitches twice now. She's the reason for every gray hair on my head. Molly, well, she's a princess. She loves pink and baby dolls. She's so outgoing whereas Daisy is shy and reserved with strangers. I don't think Molly has ever met a stranger in her short little life."

I smile to myself, thinking about how different my children are but how very much alike they are as well.

"I find them sleeping in the same bed every morning. It's usually Molly in Daisy's bed. I don't think that she can sleep without her sister. School is going to be so interesting."

I rest my head against my sister's marble gravestone, and let the world and the hours tick by. This is where I find myself, my soul, my purpose. Even though she's gone, Molly never stopped being there for me and I never stopped being there for her. We are sisters, tied together by blood, but more importantly by love.

"I miss you, Molly. I really miss you."

With a heavy sigh, I stood and pressed a kiss to my hand, placing it on the cold marble. As I turned to walk away, I knew that this wouldn't be my last time here but right now, I needed to be home with my husband and my girls. That was where I found my peace and I needed that peace now more than ever.

Made in the USA
Middletown, DE
17 August 2024